THEY'RE OUT TO GET YOU

VOLUME ONE:
ANIMALS AND INSECTS

Created and edited by
Johnny Mains

This book is dedicated to the memory of my dog, Biscuit Mains (2005-2021).

Good boy.

Biscuit Mains

TABLE OF CONTENTS

INTRODUCTION

Johnny Mains

ONE OF MY favourite nooks in the horror genre is "when animals attack" and growing up there were many treasures to be had when it came to reading material.

Ones that set me on my way were Shaun Hutson's *Slugs*, Evelyn Louise Nace's *Eat Them Alive* (written under the pseudonym Pierce Nace), Cliff Twemlow's *The Pike*, James Herbert's *The Rats*, Stephen King's *Cujo*, Mark Sonders' *Blight* and Guy N. Smith's *Night of the Crabs*.

It's the thought that normally docile animals, or even tiny creatures that normally do no more than nip or give a wee bite, can maim and kill in the most gruesome ways imaginable.

Then I started to get into the short stories in a big way, and discovered such fine fare as Oscar Cook's "Boomerang", Basil Copper's "The Spider", Erckmann-Chatrain's "The Crab Spider", John Burke's "Lucille Would Have Known", Alan Temperley's "Love on the Farm", Harry E. Turner's "The Tunisian Talking Ferret" and of course, the start of the show, George Fielding Eliot's "The Copper Bowl".

These stories (and many, many more) would see me collect as many books on the subject as I could get my hands on – and even though I sadly no longer own those books, it makes me very happy indeed whenever I come across a story or a book that's "red in tooth and claw".

So, to this anthology. Me and it were made for each other. It's as simple as that. A pulp horror fun-fest with a sprinkling of fancy writing on top. I've asked some of the best authors working in the field today and some new authors making their debut to supply me a story that will make me cheer – and they haven't let me down – so whether it's killer deer, lice, badgers, spiders, cows, dogs or pigeons, we've got you covered.

Let the carnage begin!

**—Johnny Mains,
October, 2021**

DREAM FOX

Rosalie Parker

IT HAD BEEN a fine day, warm and sunny, the insect murmur which begins in late spring becoming ever more insistent as the afternoon wore on. When the evening light had waned and twilight settled over the farm the fox family emerged from its earth at the edge of the wood. Five unweaned cubs stretched and yawned and tumbled over each other, never straying far from the watchful vixen. After sniffing the air and leaving his scent on a clump of grass, the dog fox trotted off in search of rabbits. The big fox's sleek fur and bright eyes, the alert, healthy vixen and the vigorous play of the cubs, were all pointers to his prowess as a hunter. He slinked soundlessly along the hedge until he spotted a fat doe-rabbit grazing complacently next to a molehill. She would do nicely . . . for starters. He steadied himself on his haunches, then sprang forward for the kill.

Alison trained her red plastic binoculars on the fox babies, chuckling as they play-fought and chased their own bushy tails. She was kneeling precariously on the window seat in her bedroom, trying to be quiet because she was supposed to be asleep. Downstairs, she could hear raised voices, so it was unlikely that her parents would come to check on her. Through the toy field glasses she saw the father fox arrive back at the earth, carrying a limp rabbit in his jaws, which he presented to the mother before loping back towards the fields. The vixen tore hungrily into the furry corpse and soon only scraps remained, the little foxes sniffing round where it had lain. Being a farmer's daughter, Alison was unsentimental about rabbits: they ate the grass grown for sheep and cattle to feed on. In other years, when rabbit numbers had increased to the point where they became an intolerable pest, her father would go out with his shotgun and her mother would fill the freezer, and there would be laughter and rabbit pie for dinner.

The voices downstairs grew louder, the words decipherable. There was the sound of something being smashed, then an unnatural calm before the almost-as-noisy making-up would begin. Alison, still watching the fox cubs, reasoned that because foxes ate mainly rabbits and therefore kept the population down, her father should tolerate, even welcome them. But he said foxes were a menace around the young lambs born on the farm in the early spring, although as far as she was aware a lamb was rarely taken. Sometimes her father would try to shoot a fox, but in Alison's recollection he always missed, or failed to find one to shoot at. "Reynard seems to know I'm coming," he'd say on those occasions. He called all male foxes Reynard – as his own father had.

Stars were appearing in the darkening sky. The vixen groomed her babies, licking each one all over with her rough, cleansing tongue. Stifling a yawn, Alison put down the binoculars and swung her legs over the window seat. It was quiet; time to get into bed. Pulling the covers up to her chin she dropped off to sleep and almost immediately fell into a dream. Lately, she often dreamed of the foxes. This time the mother and father fox, dressed in red hunting coats, white

Regency-style stocks and bow ties, invited her into their below-ground home. In a cavernous, earth-walled dining room the five beautifully behaved cubs sat round a table set with silver, fine china and crystal. The vixen brought in a huge rabbit pie. "You'll find no roast lamb here!" she said to Alison, who nevertheless caught an exchange of glances between the two adult foxes. Showing off their exquisite table manners, the fox cubs tucked into their portions of pie. Alison was horrified to see that the table mats beneath the plates showed scenes from a fox hunt. Ruddy-faced men on large bay horses, a pack of hounds milling around their hooves, gathered outside a country inn. Stirrup cups and hunting horns were raised.

"But fox hunting is banned!" Alison ex-claimed. "These mats are horrible! Why do you have them?"

"They're family heirlooms," said the father fox, adjusting his pristine bow-tie and picking up his wine glass. "We keep them to remind us of the oppression of our ancestors. Since our only predator, the wolf, was driven to extinction in England over 400 years ago, we've been hunted by humans with packs of hounds. It has been banned, but it still happens in some out -of-the-way places. There are men and women who enjoy the so-called sport of seeing us torn to pieces. I'd rather be finished off by a nice clean shot in the head any day of the week." He drank down the blood red contents of his glass.

Alison put down her knife and fork and hung her head. "My father tried to shoot you," she said.

The vixen sighed. "You are not your father, Alison. If you take over the farm you'll be able to do as you wish."

Alison, astonished, said, "Will the farm be mine?" This had never occurred to her, or been mentioned by her parents, even when Father let her accompany him on his frequent rounds of the fields and barns, sheep and cattle. Lately, he'd mostly forgotten to ask her along and gone out on his own.

"You're an only child," said the vixen, "so it's likely that the farm will be yours. But it probably won't happen until you've grown up and had children of your own."

"I'm not my father; I won't try to shoot you. Ever," said Alison. "And I won't let anyone hunt on my land." She stabbed her fork repeatedly into the table mat, gouging out chunks of the offending image. The little fox cubs cheered and waved their forks in the air. "Tally-ho!" cried father fox, as one by one the jolly huntsmen were mutilated beyond repair.

The cool morning breeze wafted through the partly open window, ruffling the curtains and ushering in the new day. Alison leapt out of bed and pulled on her clothes. Through the glass she could see her father on his quad bike riding over the home field towards the wood where the foxes had their earth. She watched anxiously as the bike crawled onwards over the bumpy ground, skirting the trees, apparently heading for the far barn where the cattle overwintered. As far as she could see through her binoculars, her father did not have his shotgun with him. She breathed a sigh of relief.

The vixen and her cubs slept on, curled in a bundle, the dog fox apart, waking from time to time to test the air. Inside the earth it was snug and warm, easy to slide into complacency, lower your guard. He tensed as he recognised the thrum of the quad bike nearing the wood, then relaxed, muscle by muscle, as the noise slowly receded. They were safe—for now. He felt the first stirrings of hunger and fell back into an uneasy sleep, dreaming as so often of futile chases after preternaturally speedy rabbits across the home field. Only this time the girl from the farm was at a window of the farmhouse, watching him as, straining every tendon, he miraculously caught all the dream rabbits one by one. When he woke he sensed that he had slept longer than he had meant to. It was twilight and time to wake his family and leave the earth. Tonight, there would be a full moon. He felt odd, wary, as if something or someone was waiting for him.

Alison sat patiently in the window until the foxes emerged. She thought that she would never tire of watching the cubs; even the young lambs gambolling in the fields were nowhere near as engaging. The fox father was off hunting again. She saw him give a wide berth to the huddle of ewes guarding their lambs, the mothers stamping their feet in warning as they sensed his presence. As he trotted into the home field he seemed for a moment to look up at Alison's window. She held her breath, eyes wide in the hope that he might acknowledge her, but he was quickly away, chasing a rabbit, snapping at its hind legs as it zig-zagged back to the safety of its burrow.

Then her bedroom door was being quietly opened and her mother looked in and thundered:

"What do you think you're doing? It's school tomorrow. You should be asleep!"

Alison climbed quickly into bed and closed her eyes.

"I should think so!" her mother said crossly, and shut the door. Alison followed her mother's footsteps as she stomped down the stairs.

The voices from below seeped through the floorboards. Her parents probably didn't realise she could hear them. They were arguing again about money, or the lack of it: about how badly the farm was doing and how they would have trouble paying off the bank loan. With a sickening jolt Alison realised that if they couldn't make the farm pay they would have to sell up. In her young life she had not thought that she might have to live somewhere else. She began to sob quietly, and it was a while before she drifted into an uneasy sleep.

She was standing next to the foxes' earth and the vixen was at the entrance in her hunting jacket, its brass buttons tarnished, the red cloth dirty and torn. The cubs cowered behind her.

"He's dead," the vixen said sorrowfully.

"Who?" asked Alison, fear clutching her stomach.

"Your father shot Reynard," said the vixen. "In the home field. I will have to bring up these little ones alone." She closed her eyes and hung her head. "We thought you were our friend. We hoped you would help us."

"I *am* your friend!" sobbed Alison. "But I can't stop Father. He's so much bigger than me."

The vixen sighed. "Reynard never took a lamb. Well, hardly ever. Only the stragglers. He was a good provider."

Alison reached out and stroked the red-brown fur on the fox's head.

"I don't like being me. I wish I was a fox cub."

The vixen opened her eyes and looked at

Alison thoughtfully. "Perhaps there's a way you can help us. "

When Alison arrived home from school, her father was cleaning his shotgun in the kitchen. There was a box of cartridges and a flask of oil on the table. Her mother, he said, was still in town, buying groceries for the week ahead.

"And a pretty penny she's costing me," he grumbled, wiping the oily rag up and down the barrel of the gun. "I've been meaning to talk to you, Allie. We're going to have to draw in our horns. You can do your bit and stop going to those fancy dance lessons of yours. We can't afford it. And you'll have to help on the farm. You're old enough now. It's time you toughened up and learnt what's what. Things will need to change around here. And the first thing I'm going to do is get rid of those foxes. They've been a thorn in our side for too long."

Alison said, "Why is it so important that you kill the foxes?"

"It's my land. I should be the one in charge."

Alison thought for a moment, then said, "I'll come with you, Dad."

He looked up and smiled. "Okay, love, that's grand. Be ready at dusk. Wear something dark and bring a scarf."

Satisfied that the gun was properly prepared he closed it with a clunk.

Riding pillion on the quad bike was uncomfortable and Alison had to hold on with her arms around her father's waist so as not to fall off. He balanced the shotgun across the bike in front of him so he could grab it quickly if he spotted the fox.

"Old Reynard," he was saying, "comes out at this time. He'll be feeding the vixen as well as himself, so he'll need to hunt every night. He's a cunning old boy, and keeps out of my way, but I've seen him, usually when I don't have my gun. He's a big 'un all right. I reckon we can get him if we're quiet. We'll wait in the field. There's no breeze so he'll have trouble smelling us. When we've dealt with him we'll find the earth and shoot the vixen and cubs."

"Do we *need* to kill all the foxes?" Alison asked, as evenly as she could.

"It's them or us, Alie. Times are hard. It's been a bad year and I can't afford to lose any more lambs. You're not wimping out, are you?"

"No." Alison could smell the gun oil on him, along with the scent of the gel he used in his hair. Remembering some of their happy times she rested her head on his broad back.

"We'll leave the bike here. Be really quiet from now on, Alie. And give me a nudge if you see old Reynard."

They positioned themselves beside the hedge, halfway between the wood and the rabbit burrows. It was nearly dark and the moon had risen, casting its soft glow over the field. Her father was wearing a balaclava and he had made Alison wrap the scarf around her head until only her eyes were visible. The loaded shotgun lay over his left arm, his right hand was poised on the stock. Despite the darkness Alison was aware of her father's gradual shift into the hunter's state of hyper-alertness. She knew he was listening for every minute sound, broken twig and rustle of vegetation; noting each small movement while keeping utterly still and quiet, accustoming his eyes to the dim light like a bomber pilot on a raid.

Reynard knew that hunting rabbits would be difficult in the light of the full moon. It would be better to head for the chicken coop behind the farm where he could probably find a way to dig under the wire and steal a hen or two before the panicking birds alerted the farmer to his presence. He picked up his pace across the field. It was almost time to wean the cubs. In future there would be five more hungry mouths to feed. He needed to up his game.

Hurrying on, distracted by his thoughts, Reynard nearly discounted the trail of scent which crossed his route to the coop, but his instincts kicked in and he made himself track back and check it. Mixed with the scent of two humans was a peculiar mineral smell that he could not immediately place. One of the humans was the farmer, the other was younger, and female. Sniffing the still air, he felt the fur on the back of his neck stand up. They were somewhere close, he was certain of it, but he couldn't be sure exactly where. His instincts were telling him to flee, but he knew he could not outpace the pellets from the farmer's gun.

Alison's limbs were growing heavy with the effort of keeping still. Her father was lost in the place where only the hunter and the hunted exist and time dragged on as she waited for something to happen. She watched the satellite moon on its path across the night sky, jumped a little when an owl screeched and glided down onto the grass. Occasionally a ewe bleated. Slowly, she felt something change, and she became aware of all the little movements and sounds and smells, felt all the power and mystery of the night.

Somewhere out there, was Reynard.

Her father laid his hand gently, carefully, on Alison's arm. *He's here,* she thought, but though she peered into the darkness she could not see the fox with her weak human eyes. She heard the clunk of the shotgun being readied, her father holding his breath as he raised the firearm to his shoulder—

"No!" she shouted, and nudged his arm as he fired; the barrel twitched to the side and he cursed as the shot echoed uselessly around the field. The blow came soon after and stung horribly, her cheek colouring quickly into a bruise.

"What did you do that for you stupid little bitch?"

Her father raised the gun to his shoulder and prepared to fire the other barrel. The dog fox was on him in a flash, leaping and tearing at the flesh of his trigger hand. The man yelled with fright and pain and dropped the shotgun on the grass. Alison picked up the gun and aimed it at the farmer; Reynard lay down in the grass at her feet.

"Now you know what it feels like," she said to the farmer as the red-brown fur began to sprout, first on her neck and back. The man put his hands out, palms up.

"I'm sorry I struck you, Alie," he said carefully. "Remember what I said. It's them or us."

She squeezed the trigger and felt a stab of pain as the stock thudded into her shoulder. The top half of the farmer's head exploded. The rest of him slumped to the ground, his shattered skull leaking porridgey brains onto the grass.

Alison wriggled out of her clothes and shook her herself from her pointed nose to the tip of her bushy tail. Reynard stood up.

"Well done Alison," he said, trotting off towards the wood. She limped along behind him, her right foreleg still smarting from the recoil. "Come and meet the rest of the family," he said.

A TASTE FOR PASTE

Aliya Whiteley

JAN MACKIE DELIVERED things. Generally, she had no interest in what she delivered: flowers on Valentine's Day, or gifts in merry paper bearing bows at Christmas. Toys to the kids and wine to the middle class – she treated all goods with the same quick, easy attitude. *Get it done and move on.* If the flowers lost a few petals and the gifts got a little dented, well, she wasn't being paid enough to be a perfectionist, and making deliveries had never been her dream.

Her dream was to be rich.

She didn't know how to get rich. She only knew she could have made an excellent go of it, if she was ever allowed to try. Lounging around in silk pyjamas, maybe, and having opinions on art and yachts. Telling servants to fetch things; she could have nailed that. Jan suspected she'd never get the chance. But it was, she thought, the reason why she was so fascinated by Lady Edith Frilty.

Lady Frilty had received the same delivery every Friday night since Jan first started the job, made to a grand old stately home a few miles off the M40. It was always the last box Jan dropped off before heading back to Slough and treating herself to a drink or two in the upmarket wine bar. She would sit on the last stool in the row and think about that pillared gateway, and the gravel drive that led to a big blue front door with an iron knocker.

The parcel – a box that would have held nothing larger than a toaster, say – was as light as a feather. So light that she sometimes thought it held nothing at all. It had to be signed for every single week, without exception, and so in bad weather Jan was sometimes asked to come in, and stand on the purple rug in the elegant hallway. Then a man, perhaps a bit younger than her but with a pleasant, professional manner and sexy eyes, would sign the sheet, and maybe smile, and make a comment about the weather. She assumed he was a butler or something, and he fitted into her dream very nicely.

Then the box was taken from her until the following week.

It was the only box Jan wondered about.

What was in there?

She didn't care for her job, but she was not stupid enough to risk it. She wouldn't open the box. She wouldn't even pick at the tightly sealed top flap. The sheet said it came from overseas. Sometimes, at the wine bar, she dreamed of being overseas to make a change from picturing the house. In her head it was lush jungle, exotic flowers. Could the box contain flowers? Orchids, perhaps, delicate and enticing? But no, she delivered orchids sometimes and they were always in a small basket wrapped in cellophane, displayed to the world, so that everyone could be envious of the receiver. Nobody kept flowers in a sealed box.

Jan finished her latest glass of wine, sighed, and gently stumbled home, back to her one-bedroom flat on Groundwell road. She thought about getting chips on the way back but decided against it. She had a theory that rich people did not eat chips, and restraining herself made her feel one step closer to her dream. Maybe, just maybe, the opportunity would come along to dress in those silk pyjamas and get served by that butler. If it did, she wanted to be one hundred per cent ready for it.

Friday night. The weather was momentous.

A clap of thunder, then a fast stroke of lightning, like the cut of a knife through the clouds. Hail followed, hard and unrelenting on the roof and windscreen of the van. Jan drove the last hundred metres of the road with the wipers on full, then made the usual turn and crept up the drive to Frilty Manor. She parked up, grabbed the box and the paperwork from the seat beside her, and made a dash for that blue front door. One, two, raps of the iron knocker, and the door swung open, wide. There he was, and he said, "Please, come in, come in," as if he had been waiting for her, standing on the other side, poised to allow her admittance.

Jan stood on the purple carpet as he signed the sheet, aware she was dripping. How handsome he was. Well, perhaps a little thin for her taste, but nothing some eating out wouldn't fix. He was dressed in white shirt and grey trousers, the collar a little open, revealing his Adam's Apple. She wished she was dressed in something glamorous. If only she could have met him down the wine bar – ha! As if he'd be caught dead in such a place.

"Thanks," she said, as he returned the sheet and took the box from her hands. She turned to go.

"No, no, it's still terrible out there. Please, wait for the worst to pass," he said.

"Thanks," she said again, and stood there, feeling odd, strained. Her dreams hadn't involved actually talking to him for any length of time.

"Can I ask you something?" he said, suddenly, intently.

"Sure."

"Would you like a cup of tea?"

It was so unexpected, so completely outside of the bounds of anything she thought he'd ever ask her, that it shocked her into silence.

"Or something stronger," he said. "But you're driving, I know. That's why I said tea. But I could do coffee. Or even a brandy, why not, I mean, you must be cold in those wet things . . ." He blushed violently, the bright red cheeks from nowhere a revelation. He was nervous. Around her.

"Actually, I'd love a cuppa," she said.

"Marvellous!" The blush redoubled. He said, "I mean, great, follow me, follow me," and he led her further into the grand hall, where the walls held a row of paintings in old and ornate frames, each one a portrait with haughty nose and hooded eyes. He reached a doorway, ushered her through to a large drawing room with a vast, squashy sofa and armchairs arranged around a stone fireplace so large she could have stood in it. An enveloping heat emanated from the embers of what must have been a blaze an hour or so before; the air was uncomfortably stuffy, the smell of smoke strong in her nostrils.

These dark red walls bore tapestries showing faded scenes, abstract triangles layered over each other in various colours. What did they represent? She couldn't tell. But she felt certain that they meant something to the owner, as did this room. It was well-lived in, and that meant she was a trespasser.

"Is Lady Frilty away?" she said.

A cough, like the bark of a small dog, sounded from the armchair closest to the fire, its winged back facing her.

"Lady Frilty is present," said an old voice. An amused voice.

Jan froze.

"Take a seat. Take a seat. I want to talk to you. Nigel, off you go. Make tea. Is there cake? Not that shop-bought rubbish."

"I made scones," he said, humbly. Nigel. Jan hadn't put him down as a Nigel.

"My favourite," said the voice, and Nigel turned and left without even a glance in her direction. This had been a plan – to lure her into this room, into Lady Frilty's presence. But why? And why complain? Free tea, free cake. She could hear the storm outside, battering the house. Why not stay, and enjoy the benefits of rich lifestyle, at least for the length of a cup of tea?

She walked to the armchair opposite, settled herself into it, and got her first look at Lady Frilty.

Lady. Such a grand title for such a small, folded creature. Her hair was a startling white and she bore the hooded eyes Jan had seen in the portraits. Jan wondered how many years the old woman had been sitting in this room, day after day, ordering tea and cake. She gave the impression of being immoveable in that chair, ensconced until the day they would take her out in a box.

"Do I look so very ancient?" she said.

"No, I–"

"Well you look improbably young to me. Nigel told me you were the healthy sort. A glow about you. Vigorous. He said you practically bound up to the door every Friday."

"You're always my last delivery," Jan said. "And the box is really light."

"Yes, it is, isn't it? What's your name?"

"Jan."

"Short for . . . Janet? Well, Janet, you're a godsend. I have a proposition for you. It pertains to the boxes you deliver so efficiently. And to my grandson, Nigel."

As if on cue, Nigel reappeared, pushing a silver trolley to the space between the two chairs. It was laden with a large china teapot, cups, sugar cubes, and a bowl containing some flavour of dark jam, or perhaps a shredded marmalade; it was difficult to tell in the dim light. And scones, plump and floury. It looked like Nigel was a good baker as well as a dutiful grandson.

He poured tea, steaming, from the pot, and handed her a cup with an appealing solemnity. Then the same for Lady Frilty, followed by the scones, one each – curiously dry, with no offer made of a spoonful of the jam. Jan watched as Lady Frilty lifted the entire scone to her puckered mouth and took a hefty bite. It wasn't how Jan had pictured the rich having their cake and eating it. *But if you have it, you can eat it however you want,* Jan thought, and followed suit. She washed down the crumbly consistency with the tea, which was vaguely floral.

"That will be all, thank you, Nigel," said Lady Frilty, once her mouthful was finished. Nigel obeyed the order, although this time Jan fancied he gave a guilty glance in her direction.

"And now I will tell you a story," said Lady Frilty, "and you will listen carefully."

Jan nodded. How hot the room was, and how heavy the scone was in her stomach. She hoped the story wouldn't take long.

I would like to regale you with the geographical details of my travels as a young woman; all the world was a jungle back then, at least to me, and I could find a thousand places to lose myself. My family has had money since the rise of the revolution, when machines took over the work of men, and we made our money in great factories for the exploitation of materials. I had no interest in any of it. I only cared for the natural environments that I knew were about to be reduced, bent to the will of humanity. Perhaps I was a soothsayer, of a kind. In any case, it was a pleasing irony, how I used the profits from that terrible business to journey to the very places that were being destroyed.

I saw many things that will never be seen again. And I saw other things that I am not prepared to lose. I saw life, life as a great and vigorous battle. Not in the magnificent beasts, such as the crocodiles and tigers, who are too ferocious to find a place in the modern world, but in the smallest of creatures, who must tackle unimaginable horrors in their miniature worlds as they attempt to live just one minute longer.

Butterflies.

What an awful place the world is for them. They seem helpless, so light, so delicate. Without them the world is—

"Excuse me;" said Jan. "I have to go."

"Go where?" The look on Lady Frilty's face was all astonishment; Jan wondered if she'd ever been interrupted before. But it was the end of a long shift and the tea had gone right through her. If this was going to be a long story, a pee would be needed first.

"To the – uh – Ladies' room."

"Oh! Oh. Well then. Down the hall. Next to the kitchen."

"Thanks." Jan balanced the remains of the scone and cup on the arm of the chair and hurried out of the room, back to the grand staircase. After a bit of investigation, she found a small door set under the staircase – a pull switch lit up a tiny toilet, squashed up next to a sink. She undid her trousers and urinated with the tingling sense of being watched. What was the cause? She realised it was down to the framed photographs of giant butterflies arranged around the sink mirror and the sloping wall, with big white eyes on their bright wings. Unnerving, mesmeric, it was difficult to look away – a challenge that had to be answered by staring right back.

Yes, butterflies, the old woman had said. That was her passion. Years had been spent adventuring, watching them, capturing them on film. Personally, they gave Jan the creeps. It wasn't the wings so much as the black stick legs underneath, and the long uncurling proboscis that plugged, quivering, into hidden places. She'd been taken as a child to a zoo with a butterfly enclosure, and told by her mother to hold out a pot of sugar water for them, at arm's length. They had settled on her, touched the bare skin of her arms, searched her out with those flickering tongues, and all the while her mother had said, "Don't move! Don't move!" while taking photo after photo.

Jan shook the thought off. She pulled up her trousers and flushed. A quick wash of the hands. *Shake it off,* she said to herself, but the thought of listening to butterfly anecdotes for an hour or so was enough to make her consider heading straight for the front door.

But a glance at the open doorway on her left made her change her mind.

A large kitchen table in a dark wood, sturdy and utilitarian, was in her line of sight – and, upon it, the box she had just delivered.

It was open.

She took quiet steps towards it and hesitated at the threshold. The room was a mess: unwashed dishes stacked high in the deep sink, dirty surfaces, a cracked, weary set of appliances, and an earthy smell that bothered her. She saw several discarded cardboard boxes – ones she had delivered – piled high in the corner by the back door. A large mortar and pestle sat on the draining board next to the sink.

And Nigel.

He was standing by the sink with his back to her. His shoulders were moving oddly, heaving up and down. She realised he was crying.

Back away, she thought, but it was as if he heard her thought. He whirled around, fixed her with his intense stare. He didn't seem surprised she was there. "Hi," he said. "Hi." He wiped his marvellous eyes with the sleeve of his shirt, and moved around the table to stand close.

"You okay?"

"I thought you and grandmamma would be busy for a while," he said.

"Yeah, I guess she thought that too. Listen – what am I doing here?"

"You . . ." He swallowed, then came to stand close to her. How handsome he was, even tear-streaked. Vulnerable. "You're undone."

"What?"

His eyes flicked to her crotch. "Your trousers."

She zipped up the trousers, feeling ridiculous, compromised. "God, sorry, thanks."

"No problem."

"Well, at least it made you smile," she said.

"Thanks for that. It's rare, to be honest."

"I got that feeling. Listen – I might just go. Let Lady Frilty know–"

"No! No. Please." His desperation took her by surprise. He took a step closer. "I need you."

"For what?"

"There's not long to go. She . . ." He choked up, and on instinct she touched his cheek, felt him flinch as if human contact was a shock. Then he accepted it, leaned into it. His eyes on hers were hypnotic; all she wanted was to lean in, put her mouth where her hand lingered, then slide her lips along the blade of his jaw, and taste him, like a treat–

"Not long," he whispered, and she realised what he was talking about.

The old woman was dying.

"Just listen to her," Nigel whispered. "That's all she's asking."

Jan let her hand drop.

Be company for a dying woman for a few hours, listening to her old stories. Then what? She had a feeling there was more, and she wouldn't like it. Promising to take care of Nigel, or something like it. Well, she could take him out and get him drunk after the funeral. Help him find a flat, find a life. Maybe even a life with her in it every now and again.

There would probably be a reward, too. Yes. There was bound to be a reward. Something written into the will.

"Yeah, all right," she said, and he breathed out, long and low. "But don't leave me alone in there for too long, okay?"

"Absolutely," he said.

She glanced at the table, but he was blocking her view of the box. Could she ask him what was in it? No, it felt too presumptuous. Later, maybe. She turned and made her way back down the hallway, hoping he was watching her leave.

The heat of the drawing room hit her like a weight. She collapsed back into the armchair, ignoring Lady Frilty's acid, "May I continue? But, of course, permission was not really needed. The story was launched into once more – expeditions, adventures, scientific names and descriptions that all washed over her and made it nearly impossible to stay awake. Eventually the words swung around to butterflies again – one kind in particular, and its rare and special properties. Experiments, genetics, so on and so on. It felt like a lifetime had passed by the time Nigel returned, holding the latest box in his hands, the packing tape removed but the flaps folded over the contents.

"Excellent timing," said Lady Frilty, with satisfaction, as though her story had reached the perfect conclusion. "Give it to our guest."

For a dying woman, she's got a lot of energy for these games, thought Jan. But getting to find out what had been in the deliveries all this time was worth having to play along. She lifted the flaps to find–

She flung the box away.

It toppled from her lap and hit the carpet with a dull thud. The contents spilled out in a heap: butterflies. Dead. Their wings brittle, faded, their bodies falling to pieces, to dust. They were purplish brown, but she guessed they were once scarlet, and one element remained vivid: the eyes on the wings, bright white, with a fixed black pupil in the centre.

Nigel fell to the floor and began to gather them, his fingers nimble, returning them to the box with an uncanny speed. The job done, he took the box to the silver trolley and stored it with tender care beside the remaining scones.

"Butterfingers," said Lady Frilty. "Thousands of pounds, nearly wasted. I thought you were meant to be a competent person. That is, after all, why you are here."

"I don't get it," said Jan. Just the thought of those dead insects, piled high in the box, made her skin crawl. She had been bringing them here for months. Years.

"Were you not listening? The *Attacus argus* species of butterfly has the certain medicinal properties I have explained to you, and your regular delivery produces just enough to keep one person dosed. It has been a costly endeavour, but undoubtedly worth it."

No wonder the old woman didn't look ill. She had all the medicine she needed. "But – Nigel said you didn't have long..."

Lady Frilty chuckled. Her face was a picture of smug enjoyment. "Not me, dear. He was talking about himself. Nigel's days are numbered, you see. At least, in this body. He is, you see, quite quite special . . ."

"What?" She turned to Nigel, and found him gorging on jam, straight from the bowl, feasting upon it with an unabashed enjoyment. His fast tongue flickered in and out, flicking the stuff into his mouth. And still Lady Frilty talked, pleasure evident in her voice, as if the sight of him was deeply enjoyable.

". . . a weakling child, parents dead, given over to my care for this grand experiment, fed only on the mashed carcasses of the *Attacus argus* – and now, now! We approach the moment of transformation. He will be unique, and demanding in his desires. He will have needs for which I cannot provide, but you, you with your youth and strength, you can match this challenge –"

"It's now," said Nigel, "Now!" He doubled over, then curled up tight, tighter. She heard his vertebrae cracking, his ribs snapping, his neck breaking as his head contorted to his chest, and he folded double – then he quivered, and she could not rip her eyes away from the waxy sheen of his skin that began to seal his limbs to his torso. He was becoming a lump of flesh, the individual parts of his body merging, mutating, his clothes dissolving in an oily puddle that soaked into the old carpet and sealed him.

"He's magnificent," breathed Lady Frilty.

"It's . . ."

"A chrysalis."

The process ceased. The room was so hot, quiet.

Through the glistening coating, greenish in tone, Jan watched as something shifted, then settled back into stillness. For a moment she thought she saw a giant white eye pressed up against the inside of the chrysalis.

"Who knows how long this next stage will take? Your duties can begin immediately, Janet. Take care of me while we wait, together, and if I am dead by the time he emerges so be it. He will be your responsibility alone. I place the legacy of the Frilty family in your hands."

"What . . . What's coming out of there?"

"Did you hear nothing I said? Well, no matter. We'll have time for repetition later. For now, why don't you go upstairs and pick out a room you'd like? And think about what salary you'd command. I'll write you a generous first payment. Whatever you like, within reason. And you will, of course, inherit everything when I'm gone. With the stipulation that you continue to care for Nigel."

Jan stood up. The teacup fell from the arm of her chair to the floor. On instinct, she retrieved it, and took it to the silver trolley. Close to the chrysalis – to Nigel, she told herself – she breathed in a sharp and strange smell, like a rich perfume. It wasn't unpleasant.

"Sure," she said. "I'll pick out a room."

Out of the drawing room, down the hall, out of the front door. Into the van.

She drove slowly, carefully, not quite trusting herself, seeing the tremor of her hands on the steering wheel. *I didn't have the jam*, she told herself over and over. *I never touched that jam.* But she had touched Nigel. His handsome face. Those eyes.

Later, in the wine bar, back in her usual seat, Jan felt a little calmer. She tried to think it through without emotion.

All the money she could ever want. Her dream, made a reality.

She could sit and wait for the old woman to die. Then she could torch that thing and be done with it. Or simply walk out, and be free and rich for the rest of her life. Silk pyjamas. A beautiful butler of her own.

But if . . .

But if Nigel emerged before that time, what would he be? She ordered another glass of wine, then a third, and realised something. Under her repulsion was a strange desire to see it, to see him, come forth. Would he be majestic? Horrifying? What needs could he possibly have that she could meet?

Jan sat there, weighed her options, and wondered if she wanted to become the kind of woman who could deliver the next stage of Nigel to the world.

Fifty-Seven Years Later

"But I'm just a handyman."

". . . but that's why you're here, dear. I need someone young and strong to take over. I'm certain there's not much time to go before Nigel arrives. He'll have needs, you see. Needs that I'm just too old to meet."

"What sort of – needs?" said Ben.

"Did you not listen to what I just told you?" There was a steely quality to Mrs Mackie's voice that took Ben by surprise. How small, how harmless she looked in that squashy armchair, before the glow from the embers in that enormous fireplace. It was too hot, too dark, to concentrate on anything for long. He sat in the facing chair, feeling sweat prickle on his back and underarms. "Never mind, I can tell it to you again later. Lady Frilty told it to me often enough before her death."

Being trapped in this room, listening to the same story over and over again. What a nightmare. *Just say no*: thought Ben. *Just say no thanks, and walk out.*

But the money.

The money, the house, the life: he'd been offered it all to stay. He had always dreamed of these things since he was little, before he had realised it would never happen and got the job as a handyman at Frilty Manor last year. He'd found himself enjoying the work, and being close to real wealth, right up until the moment he'd been invited into the drawing room for the very first time and seen the thing lying on the carpet.

The lump.

The chrysalis, if he believed Mrs Mackie.

Nigel.

The old lady was crazy. This had to be a scam. But if it was a scam, what was that lump?

"I see your eyes are drawn to him. I've often found the same thing," said Mrs Mackie. "He's been my only companion for years, and he is amazing. Touch him. You'll be surprised. He won't mind."

Ben adjusted his utility belt, low around his waist. His tools were a reassuring weight. Then he moved slowly across the room. The chrysalis was in the darkest corner. On either wall, framing it, were two large tapestries of many triangular shapes, varied in colour. When he got close he realised they were, in fact, a representation of butterflies in a helix design, spinning around in space. DNA: that was what the pattern reminded him of. He remembered seeing it in a textbook in school.

"He rolled there a few months ago," said Mrs Mackie. "The excitement I felt when he moved! I thought I would die on the spot. It had been so long – I had almost given up on him. I've thought of leaving so many times, after Lady Frilty died, but I felt he was . . . dependent on me. I can't explain it. Touch him."

Ben knelt and put one hand to the surface.

It was dry. Rough under his palm. Not slimy,

even though it appeared to be a waxy surface. The warmth surprised him.

Movement.

He jerked his hand away. Even in the semi-darkness he could see something stirring within, rotating, then – an eye. Undoubtedly a large white eye with a fixed black pupil, pressed against the coating. Then another. Another. The eyes continued to appear, to fix on him. At least a dozen of them.

Rustling.

It sounded like the crackling of dead leaves. It grew louder. Louder.

A crack appeared. It widened, ran down the length of the chrysalis, and Ben saw strands of white matter inside, thick, like cobwebs. They elongated, then snapped as the opening peeled back further. A pinkish jellied substance within quivered. Pushed. Erupted outwards, hardened as it hit the warm air and became – a man. On his knees, his back curved so his face was hidden. He had matted hair, plastered to his scalp, and his spine was lumpy, twisted.

"Nigel," breathed Mrs Mackie.

The head snapped up at the sound.

No eyes. A nose and mouth, human. But only a soft grey substance, dense as cotton wool, where the eyes should be. It bulged, and two long feelers emerged, seeking out the room lightly, waving back and forth. And the twisted spine burst open, the bones of the ribcage pointing upwards, then extending to form a framework. Wings. Huge, wet wings, trembling, forming. Fluttering.

Ben could not move, couldn't find strength in his legs. The thing – Nigel – straightened, came to him. The feelers in the face stretched out, danced over his head, his shoulders.

"I'm here," said Mrs Mackie. "I've waited for you."

It moved across the room, to the chair, and the wings were magnificent, vivid red against the glow of the fire as they stretched out and the eyes, moving eyes, fixed themselves on Ben. Mrs Mackie squeaked. It bent over her, the feelers touching her mouth. The wings folded, enclosed her. The head bent forward. The armchair was almost hidden from view as she groaned, one long deep sound of – suffering? Ecstasy? Both.

"Now," she said.

The word somehow freed Ben. He pulled his hammer from his toolbelt, ran forward, brought the hammer down again and again on the pink line of the back between the wings. The thing made no sound as the skin gave under the onslaught and blood flung up, lungs exposed. The wings beat back against Ben's arms and he hit them too, in fury, in fear, until they stopped moving.

The eyes, the horrible eyes on the wings were still fixed upon him.

He pushed them away and the creature crumpled to the carpet.

In the armchair, Mrs Mackie was a shrivelled, dead thing. The shock, maybe. Or something Nigel had done to her. What had she said? It had . . . needs. It had been all over her, touching her. He had the feeling it had been trying to get inside her. Those long feelers, inside her mouth, searching, pushing.

He sat on the carpet for a while, panting, trying to breathe smoothly, slowly. Eventually he felt calm enough to wipe his hammer on the carpet, and stand up.

Had the old lady got what she wanted?

Even if she hadn't, it occurred to him that it no longer mattered. But he – he could now have what he had always wanted.

He could move into Frilty Manor, sell the old paintings and the jewels and whatever else he found upstairs. He could live in luxury for a while. He'd been there long enough to know nobody ever came to visit Mrs Mackie. It could be months before anyone worked out she was dead. Years, even.

To start with, he did what a good handyman should. He cleared up the mess.

The ugly tapestries came in handy for wrapping up the bodies, and then he dragged them both to the garden, dug a hole and buried them, one on top of the other. The eyes on the brilliant wings were already fading, turning to grey dust, as he shovelled over the dirt.

Back in the kitchen, he made himself a cup of tea and examined the contents of the fridge for something to eat. Everything looked old, as shrivelled and past its best as the old lady had. All except for a small china bowl of jam at the back of the top shelf.

Ben took it, scooped it up with his finger and put it in his mouth. It had a strong taste, but not unpleasant. He ate the whole lot, and licked the bowl clean. He wondered if there was more to be found anywhere.

He thought he could get a taste for it.

THE HUFAIDH SOUNDER

Ray Cluley

NO ONE THOUGHT too highly of the Ma'dān, and as Owens didn't think too highly of himself either he chose to stay amongst them after the war.

Physically, they weren't all that different from an Englishman. They had darker skin, of course, and darker hair they kept hidden beneath a *keffiyeh* or headcloth, but otherwise Owens thought them much the same. Many of the other Arabs hated the Ma'dān, though, considering them treacherous and violent – and many of them were – but as Owens had discovered in the four years he'd fought for King and Country, all men had dark, destructive appetites.

The Ma'dān had made enemies of both sides during the war, murdering and looting from vantage points within the marshes they knew so well. The marsh was where they lived. Seasonal marshes dried up in the autumn and winter months and temporary marshes came with the floods, but as a constant the marshes of southern Iraq gave them everything they needed, and for a while they gave Owens what he needed, too.

6,000 square miles in which to lose himself or find himself. Whichever came first.

The waterways were a maze of barely visible lanes amongst the reedbeds, but Owens' canoeboys knew where they were going. All he had to do was use the tin can in his lap to bail out the water whenever there was enough to warrant his attention – the bitumen was cracking and in need of a recoat – but even then he kept a keen eye on the reeds, watching for anything that might deserve the attention of his rifle.

Behind him, two canoes followed. Radhawi was in front. He nodded that all was well, and Owens nodded back before a comment from one of his boys brought his attention back to the path ahead.

Hatab wore his headcloth without a head-rope, twisting the cloth in place, and his shirt had been patched many times. He liked to joke his muscles tore the fabric, and that each patch and repair was a celebration of his physique: the boy was as slim as a reed. He was pointing now and the other boy, Tahir, nodded and they steered the canoe into a new channel. Previously they had been following a lane made by passing buffalo, but now they were picking out their own route by instinct. Owens had learned to trust their instincts. Even amongst the densest reeds they could find the entrance to the smallest waterway. It was a great skill, and one they were certain to need as they passed into less familiar territory. Their tracking skills, too. Hatab boasted he could track a swimming pig. Tahir that he could determine types of fish by their wake as they passed.

As if he knew he was being thought of, Tahir turned and smiled. He was trying to grow a moustache, but it was still little more than a patchy dark fuzz on his lip. He wore his hair in two long braids either side of his face.

"*Filhu*?" he asked. Stop and feed?

Owens shook his head. They had an hour or so before they'd need to think about camp. The boy patted a bag to remind Owens where the food was, should he be hungry, and returned his attention to the route.

Just as they emerged into an open area of water they discovered an abandoned canoe, half submerged on a mudflat amongst a bed of bulrushes. Owens had been cradling his rifle, but he took a firmer grip of it now as they approached. He wondered if an attempt had been made to scuttle the boat, or if it had simply been abandoned. He wondered, too, if it was a distraction. He looked left and right for an ambush but saw no one. Behind them, the other two canoes slowed to drift close.

The abandoned canoe was old. Much of it was rotten, the softer planks fallen from the ribs. It didn't belong to their man.

Nevertheless, Radhawi checked the old boat over. He retrieved a punting pole from inside, tested its strength, and discarded it into the reeds.

It was enough to startle a heron from some hidden spot. It shook itself from cover and took to the sky with a sudden beating of its great wings.

Owens raised his rifle and fired and the bird fell, wings folded around itself and legs trailing behind. An easy shot, but the others praised his reflexes.

"What do you want to do, *sahib*?" Radhawi asked.

Sahib. Friend. Killing something always made you a firmer friend of the Ma'dān. Owens looked at the bank and thought it a suitable place. "*Filhu*," he said.

Stop and feed.

The tent was warm with the light of a hurricane lamp, and with the heat rising from the men. The smell of the mud and reeds beneath their mats, together with the odour of damp clothes drying, leant the heat a cloying, earthy moistness that wasn't altogether unpleasant. The tent was black goat hair and that held its own smell too, but it was the aroma of heron cooking outside that Owens focussed on. Heron was a good meal, providing as much meat as a sheep but with a stronger flavour. It would make a welcome change to the fish and rice they had been eating for the last three days.

The men had taken off their cloaks, and the cartridges of their bandoliers caught the lamplight, glinting in lines like deadly constellations. Each man sat with their rifle in their lap or held upright beside them as they talked. One of the men was eying Owens's weapon with open interest.

"Khalaf, isn't it?"

The man nodded.

Owens passed Khalaf his rifle. He had sold his standard army issue Lee-Enfield shortly after the war and replaced it with a .275 Rigby which, with its moderate recoil, superior range, and excellent penetration, was better for hunting. He asked for Khalaf's opinion. The men he met on the marshes were always keen to talk about rifles.

Khalaf looked the weapon over and simply said, "Good." When he handed it back, he drew the knife he wore at his belt for Owens to admire in turn, his rifle being no better than anyone else's. The blade was narrow and curved and wickedly sharp. Many of the Ma'dān carried such knives, but Owens nodded and said, "Good," and Khalaf seemed pleased.

"It was my father's," he said. "It was stolen from him. I had to kill to get it back." His smile was wide and without menace. He simply wanted to be recognised as worthy for their venture, and Owens gave him the validation by clasping his shoulder and nodding.

The man they were tracking had also stolen a weapon. More than that, he had killed a woman. He'd claimed he thought her a wild pig and fired before he was certain, killing her by accident, and he'd pleaded inexperience with the rifle he'd borrowed to protect his crops, but the hows and whys of what had happened were not important. Amongst the Ma'dān, a killing could only be appeased by another death or recompensed with *fasl*. Blood money. The man they were tracking had refused to pay the *fasl* and fled.

The sad truth of it was that more value was placed upon the stolen rifle than the *fasl* for a dead woman.

Owens returned Khalaf's knife and excused himself to check on the food. He took his rifle with him.

Outside, two of the boys were repairing the canoe he'd been travelling in. They were heating the bitumen with a reed torch to seal the cracks, a temporary measure until the boat could be recoated. The smell of hot tar was thick and Owens turned away from it as he passed to stand upwind. Stars were shyly emerging in the purple of the sky. The moon was close to full, marking another month in the company of marshmen, and Owens did not know when he would leave. When he'd told his Captain of his plans to stay after the war, the man had joked that Owens was only happy when scratching fleas from his shirts and chest hair. He had bid Owens, "*Salam alaikum,*" peace be on you, and Owens shook the man's hand with, "*Alaikum as salam,*" on you be peace, but peace was no longer something Owens believed in. The war had done that to him. He had seen men do terrible things, had done terrible things. Men barely more than boys had become animals in battle, slaughtering and being slaughtered, and Owens couldn't go home after that. Something in him had changed, and he didn't know yet if it would change back. Or if he wanted it to.

A quiet noise behind him had him turn with rifle raised, but it was only Hatab. He was carrying a platter of meat to the tent.

Owens lowered his weapon and followed the boy back.

"He has returned!" Radhawi announced, and said to the man next to him, "You must tell him about Hufaidh after we have eaten."

The name sounded familiar to Owens, but he couldn't recall where he'd heard it, and he was too hungry to think about it now. He sat back amongst them and they washed their hands then ate in silence. They ate the heron with disks of bread that tasted of the ashes they'd been cooked in. Afterwards they ate hard yellow cakes made from the pollen of bulrushes. Owens had grown to like the taste. When they drank, Owens offered his cup to Radhawi who laughed at the familiar joke between them, and he offered it to the other men who laughed as well. They would not drink from the same cup as an infidel.

One of the men spat and said, "English pig!" and Owens laughed with him.

"That is Barur," Radhawi said. "Don't listen to what he says. When a child dies very young, his brother is given an unpleasant name to ward off the evil eye, but Barur was named for how he looked."

Barur snatched up his rifle and aimed it at Radhawi, who laughed and took cover behind one of the canoeboys.

"Barur," Owens said, "that means dung?"

Barur turned his threat on Owens, brandishing his rifle with his eyes wide and mouth open in mock rage.

"Save my sahib from Barur, Hashim," Radhawi said. "Tell him about when you went to Hufaidh."

Radhawi had redirected his joking, it seemed, for now the men laughed at the one called Hashim.

Hashim smiled. "I have not been to Hufaidh," he said, "but I may have met a man who had."

To Owens, Radhawi said, "It is said, that no man can look upon Hufaidh and remain wise in his mind."

"What is this place?"

"It is an island," Hashim said.

"It is a legend," said Sabaiti.

Hashim nodded as if it could be both. "There is a great palace, and there are palm trees. The buffalo there are big, much bigger than in any of the marshes." He gestured, measuring a height above his head. "But anyone who sees the place is cursed and can speak no sense. Their words are spoken out of order and no one can understand them."

"Then how do we know about the palace and the palm trees and the buffalo?" Radhawi asked. Owens smiled, and a few of the men chuckled quietly, but most were listening closely to Hashim, though they had surely heard such stories many times. Owens had heard it spoken of before, he realised. A great sheikh had searched for it with a whole fleet of canoes. It was a story he'd heard told by way of an insult of one of the tribes, and someone told it again now.

Hashim shook his head. "The *Jinns* hide the island."

Nobody joked at this. Someone explained to Owens that Jinns were malevolent spirits or shapeshifting demons, and he nodded as if he believed them.

"Hufaidh cannot be found unless the Jinns will it to be so," Hashim said. "And those who find it do not easily leave, though I once traded some food for an idol that the owner claimed had come from Hufaidh. The man was... not wise in his mind. But I could understand his words. He said the idol was given to him as protection, but he was in more need of food so I traded with him."

Hashim paused, and perhaps it was for dramatic effect, but to Owens it seemed the man was struggling with how to proceed.

"It was strange to look at," he said eventually. "It was awful and it was pleasing."

"Let us see it."

"I did not like to look at it. At first I liked it, but then . . ." He shook his head. "It was made of lead. I melted it to make bullets."

Of course, Owens thought. Bullets were also awful and pleasing.

"What happened to the man?" Sabaiti asked, but Hashim didn't know.

"When I traded with him, we were not far from here," he said.

"Perhaps he went back to Hufaidh."

"Perhaps it is close by."

"Maybe the man we seek has found it and hides from us there," Owens said. He was joking but the men nodded as if it were possible.

"We will find him, wherever he is," said Radhawi. "The Jinn will not hide *him*."

After that, the talk turned to other things, but later, as they spread qasab mats and goatskins for sleep, Owens' mind returned to Hufaidh and strange idols, and he wondered if he would dream, but he did not.

They found their man early the next day.

At first their progress was slow. The qasab grew tall and close, the tasselled stems as thick as punt-poles and full of shadows, and moving through it was arduous work, but eventually the channel opened into a wide lagoon. Several small islands were gathered at the furthest end. These were *tuhul*, some of them anchored but most of them free to drift across the water, floating islands that were masses of qasab and brambles.

"Sahib," said Radhawi, and when he had Owens's attention he pointed to one of the larger islands, where a canoe had been pulled up amongst the reeds. It was not rotted like the last one they'd found, and inside with the paddles and punt-pole was a cloth bag of supplies. No rifle, though. Wherever he was, he had it with him.

The men moved quietly, drawing their canoes up onto the *tuhul*.

Tuhuls were made of layers of roots and rotting vegetation, and though the ground of it looked solid enough you would sink through if you stood too long in one place. Owens moved into a thicket of willow bushes, stepping over and around clumps of sedge and keeping himself low. With Radhawi to the right of him, he focussed his attention to the left, his rifle held down at his side but hands positioned ready to raise and fire at once. The ground was wet underfoot, spongy, and it was easy to see where someone had passed, trampled grasses and broken stems of qasab pointing the way.

Owens knelt at where a bottle had been dropped. A wick of cloth had been pushed into the neck and dates, squashed in around it, held it in place. An improvised lamp, still sloshing with paraffin and never lit. He showed it to Radhawi then tucked it inside his shirt, leaving both hands free again for his rifle.

The next thing they found was a rolled tent tied with cord and half submerged in the 'ground' of the island. The path from there was even easier to follow, the route so clear that Owens suspected a trap of some kind, but before he could say anything to Radhawi the man stopped. He did it so abruptly that Owens snapped his rifle up to shoot, but no enemy presented itself.

Radhawi turned to look at him and shook his head.

"We have found him," he said, and parted more of the reeds for Owens to see.

A small area had been trampled flat, and mats laid down as if readying for camp, though to camp on a *tuhul* would have been beyond foolish. It would have been dark, Owens allowed, thinking of the lamp. And perhaps he was frightened, not thinking straight.

Looking at the dead man sprawled in the reeds confirmed the frightened part.

The man lay sprawled at a stand of reeds and brambles, his legs splayed and seemingly gone from the knees down, sunk into the base of the *tuhul*. His arms were open wide, hooked around the reeds to keep the rest of him upright. He'd been eviscerated, his stomach opened to spill stinking strings of intestine onto his thighs.

Owens fancied he could see them steaming still, in the morning air. He'd seen a man shredded open like this in the war, strung on wire, but that man's face had been a contortion of pain. This man had died in fear. Many do, Owens knew. He'd seen them surprised by death then frightened by what might come after, but this man . . .

"His face," said Hashim.

The others had gathered with them, a dozen men looking at one whose face was gaunt with horror, his mouth an open, hanging pit. There was no vacancy in the look of his wide, wild eyes. It was as if they still beheld the terror of dying.

Radhawi squatted to retrieve a rifle lying across the dead man's lap. Guts snaked from where they were draped over the barrel and spooled into the marsh. He inspected it. "Not been fired." He wiped the weapon and gave it to Sabaiti, who looked it over and nodded.

"*Fasl* has been paid," he said.

"Look at his hand," said Owens. "His right hand."

It was bloody, coated to the wrist. In the reeds beside him was his knife. The curved blade and much of the hilt was also bloody.

"He fought back," said Radhawi.

Owens shook his head. "I don't think so."

"He got them," Radhawi said, and mimed a slash and thrust as if gesturing would make his claim more convincing, but Owens said no. "What then, sahib? Tell me."

Before he could say anything, the spongy ground seemed to tremble and the reeds around them shuddered before parting with an eruption of movement. A bristling, snorting mass of muscle thundered into Radhawi and knocked him down before tossing one of the canoeboys aside. It struck Owens, too, but as he spun with the impact he brought his rifle to bear on the creature.

It was a boar, standing four feet high and as long as a man was tall, and it turned to barrel through them again.

One of the men cried out as he fell, clutching at his side. Another was struck to the ground and trampled.

Owens couldn't shoot – there were too many men he might hit now he'd turned – but he saw Sabaiti raise his retrieved rifle and fire just as the pig slammed into him. The rifle went high, and Owens felt a hammer blow to his chest that seemed to smash his ribs like glass. It knocked him to the ground. Tahir, beside him, fell too.

Men cried out warnings and panicked instructions as the pig moved amongst them, and Owens heard at least two more shots as he felt carefully at his wound. He could feel sharp fragments of bone splitting out from his skin, but when he looked down he didn't see shards of bone but pieces of broken bottle protruding from his shirt. He was wet with paraffin, not blood. The bullet had struck the lamp he'd been carrying.

Tahir had fallen beside him and Owens checked him and saw a quarter of the boy's face was gone, cratered outward from the eye socket where he'd caught the ricochet. The boy twitched, not yet done with dying.

Owens grabbed his rifle. He used it to get up then pointed it left and right for its target.

The rest of the men had dispersed, spreading out as much as the space allowed, so that they stood in a loose semi-circle around the pig that ran first at one and then another of them. Owens had seen cornered animals act viciously, but this one had a clear route to flee if it wanted to. Instead, it chose to attack the men before it, focussing each time on the ones who raised their rifles. Each of them abandoned their shot to dodge the beast instead.

The Rigby was slippery in Owens's hands because his grip was slick with paraffin, but he took aim at the pig and when it came at him he was resolute. It came at him huffing and grunting and was upon him the instant he fired.

The pig squealed, a terrible high-pitched shriek. Even shot, its momentum carried it forward and it butted Owens down, tearing a line out of the man's thigh. It stumbled to its face, squealed again, and was still.

"Are you all right, sahib?"

Blood was spilling from between his fingers where he held at his wound, but he risked a look and saw it wasn't bad. It was bleeding profusely, but someone handed him a strip of bandage, and he wrapped the wound tight as others took care of wounds of their own. Another of them had been gouged like Owens. Sabaiti held his stomach, still struggling for breath. He was looking at Tahir, who stared up at the sky with one sightless eye.

Owens looked for Radhawi and saw the man squatting down at the pig. It lay on its side, blood spilling to the watery ground and puddling in the bed of the *tuhul*. Radhawi pulled back the flesh of its mouth to show Owens the curve of its tusks. "Big for a sow," he said, then noticed Tahir.

"Sabaiti," Radhawi said.

The man only glanced at him. Then he looked to his rifle and cast it aside. "It is cursed with death," he said.

That's every rifle, Owens thought, but he said nothing. It was a silence the others took up as they carried the boy back to the canoes. They took the dead man, too, and the boar as well, trussing its feet to carry over a pole.

At the canoes, a man called Badai drew their attention to several others coming to them across the lagoon. There was no question they'd been seen. The boats were heading straight for the *tuhul*.

"They heard the shots," said Radhawi.

"Whose territory is this?" Owens asked.

"There is some debate on that matter."

"Great."

Being in someone else's territory could be dangerous at any time, but if the area was contested the danger increased as either tribe would suspect them rivals.

"I think they're women," Badai said.

He was right. There were a few men, but even in the canoes of mixed sexes it was the women who were sitting in front to paddle, which was very unusual. Owens had never seen it, in fact. He pointed it out to Radhawi.

"Perhaps they are *mustarjil*," he said.

Mustarjil. Women who lived as if men, working as men. They would sit in the *mudhif* and eat with the men, and when they died they were honoured with rifle fire like men. Owens had met several before, but he'd never seen so many at once. There were a dozen of them over four boats. It would make for a well-matched fight if it came to that. *Mustarjil* also fought as fiercely as men, perhaps more so.

"*Salam alaikum!*" Radhawi called to them.

They did not reply immediately, and Owens felt the men around him tense. He knew without looking they would be holding their rifles a little harder, and a little higher, but when the women were close enough to speak rather than shout, one of them said;

"*Alaikum as salam.*"

She was punting the lead canoe which drifted now towards theirs. She said something quietly to the others in her boat before asking Radhawi, "Why are you here?"

"Hunting."

It wasn't a lie in itself, but he didn't point to the man they'd been tracking. He pointed to the boar.

The woman bristled as if she knew he was trying to deceive her, and those with her muttered amongst themselves. Again, there was tension amongst them, like a taut drumskin waiting to be struck.

Knowing he was an unusual sight in the marshes, Owens stepped forward to be seen more clearly, a distraction of sorts, but the women showed him little interest.

"Yours?" a woman asked Radhawi, and for a moment Owens thought she meant him, but she pointed to where a man and boy lay dead.

Radhawi said, "Yes. We are taking them home."

The woman nodded. Then she pointed to the boar and said, "Ours."

Two of the other women stepped into the water and went to the animal.

One of the men, Barur, began to protest, but Radhawi quickly hushed him. A pig was a small price to pay for trespassing.

As the pig was transferred from the canoe, some of the other women disembarked from theirs to take positions in those of the men, and before there could be any further protest the men were told, "You must come with us. We shall eat, and honour your dead."

They crossed the lagoon and followed a series of waterways that threaded upon themselves before opening up again into an open expanse of water. A black mound, rising gently from surrounding reeds, was their obvious destination, an island of solid ground with a natural cleft perfect for the mooring of the canoes.

As they neared, Owens saw a number of buffalo, the largest he had ever seen in the marshes. Some of them stood by the water's edge, huge, bulk-bodied animals with curved horns as thick as a man's arm. Others rested in the water with only their heads and muscled backs protruding. The women guided a sure course between them, and the canoes slid to a stop on the reeded bank. Immediately, two of the women unloaded the shot boar. They caressed the animal almost tenderly before heaving it from the canoe.

Nobody spoke. The men looked from one to the other for communication, and with the threat of hostility gone a few of them openly appraised the women anew. The women, though, went about their business as if the men weren't there, heading into the bulrushes and allowing them to follow if they so wished.

The men followed.

Yellow rushes stood like a wall around the island, and they followed a short path through to discover a cleared space where some thirty or so houses stood. Some of these were little more than rushes gathered together as a cone, much like an upended nest. Others, similarly constructed, were longer and arched like short tunnels, reed mats fitted to qasab frames and draped with animal skins and cloth.

Dominating them all was a large *mudhif.* Eighty feet in length, it had seventeen arches. A single huge mat made the roof, while others hung as panels from the roof to the ground. As the weather was warm, many of these had been propped up to leave the inside open, a vast inviting space large enough to house the whole village at once.

All around, people were busying themselves with the daily tasks of village life, and they barely acknowledged the arrival of strangers. Some were milking buffalo. Others were making small bricks of the dung to burn as fuel. At several fires, women were slapping dough onto platters, and the air was rich with the aroma of cooking bread. Owens found himself drawn to watching two women pounding grain with heavy pestles at a large mortar, and he felt a moment of shame at finding something erotic in the way they'd bend at the hips, taking turns in a rhythm of work that had them grunting and sweating. They had gathered up their long gowns and tied them shorter between their legs. One of them saw him watching, spoke to her companion, and the two of them exerted themselves all the more loudly as if to tease or provoke him.

Owens looked away.

The women they had followed into the settlement had dispersed to mingle again with their people, but one remained to lead them into the *mudhif.* It was cool beneath the roof. The pliable reeds that formed the arched columns had been decorated with henna handprint patterns. The area inside was divided into three short platforms, one of which was piled with goat hair sacks of food, folded clothing and rolls of blankets. There were carpets, and a scattering of cushions decorated the mat floor, except where a large space had been dug open for a fire.

"Rest," the woman said. "Someone will come to dress your wounds. Then you will eat with us, and we shall consummate a new friendship." She nodded to them, or perhaps it was a quick bow, and then she left.

They were not alone for long. First their wounds were cleaned and dressed, and then there was the ritual of making coffee, which was strong and bitter but restorative, and the men, despite their recent ordeal, began to relax. Part of that could be attributed to the trio of young women who sang to them. Familiar songs at first, but also songs Owens had never heard before. Several times he had to ask someone for an explanation of meaning.

"Hunting songs," Radhawi said. "They honour the boar, and they sing of feasts."

And though it must have happened gradually, it seemed to Owens that without announcement the *mudhif* was suddenly full. There were few men, surly and watchful, but the women made them feel welcome. Young boys lit lamps and hung them around the *mudhif*.

"When did it become dark?"

No one had an answer for him, although more fuel was added to the fire as if Owens' question had been a complaint, dried blocks of buffalo dung releasing their familiar, pungent odour. Grasses, too, with a sharper, less pleasant smell, were added to the flames and the smoke paled. Owens moved deeper into the mudhif to escape fumes that made his eyes water, and as he resettled more women arrived with attractive platters of honeyed treats and meat.

"Eat!"

The meat was delicious, succulent, tender chunks that fattened the rice with rich juices. Like famished men, they devoured it quickly.

"Eat," they were told again. "You will need your energy!"

Drums were fetched, and tambourines, and after the skins had been tightened over the fire there was music and the men were urged to dance.

Owens, though, felt giddy and lightheaded. Thinking it was perhaps the acrid smoke from the fire, he excused himself for some fresh air. Alcohol was forbidden amongst the Ma'dān, but he staggered from the *mudhif* like a drunk man.

Outside, night had fallen, and it felt to Owen like many hours had passed in the span of a single one. A fat moon looked down upon the marshes with her sisters the stars, and Owens hoped their cool light would do as much to clear his addled mind as the clean air. He felt strange. Like he was wading through silvered water.

The village had emptied itself into the *mudhif,* but Owens was not alone outside. A wandering buffalo paused to rub its shaggy body against one of the palm trees near the *mudhif* as if it, too, wanted to dance to the music pulsing from inside.

"There is a great palace, and there are palm trees," came a voice out of the dark.

It was Hashim.

He said, "The buffalo there are big, much bigger than in any of the marshes." He gestured, measuring a height above his head.

"You've said something like this to me before," Owens said.

Hashim nodded. He looked back at the *mudhif*. "The women here are like that idol I once owned. Pleasing to look at, but . . ."

"Dangerous," said Owens. "Like bullets."

"Yes. Like bullets." He looked at Owens. "The idol looked, in parts, like a woman."

"Which parts?" Owens asked, but Hashim said nothing else.

"Come on," Owens said. "I'm still hungry. Let's find what might be left of that boar."

But Hashim was already gone, and Owens wondered if he'd even been there at all. He wondered, too, if there had been something in the *mudhif* fire that muddled his mind and stirred his appetite. He really was very hungry.

He stumbled his way to the place he'd seen them take the boar and announced himself with, "*Salam alaikum*," at the door and, receiving no reply, entered the house thinking it empty.

It was not. In fact, he had intruded on a woman as she finished dressing. There was another with her, and she scowled at Owens as he apologised, but the woman dressing was not embarrassed or offended, and she bid him stay a moment. "You are the brave warrior," she said. "You shot the boar."

"Yes. I'm looking for it now."

"Still hungry?" She gestured the other woman away when Owens nodded, he assumed to fetch more food, but when she was gone the woman said, "A man has many appetites," and grabbed a fistful of his shirt to pull herself close and put her mouth to his. Owens pushed back before it became a kiss and she retreated willingly, but she held his hand where he'd placed it on her and after a moment lowered it to her breast and moved close again and this time he did not force her away. Women who engaged in sex before they were married were killed to restore a family's honour, but Owens thought of this only briefly when she put her hands into his trousers and pulled at him with eager skill. Perhaps with no fathers or brothers here to punish them, the women had no fear. Perhaps the lack of men heightened appetites of their own.

She used one hand on him and pulled at her own gown with the other, bunching it up around her waist. He felt the coarse hair of her crotch against him where the nakedness of their bodies touched and he felt the heat of her on his skin and then she was urging him down upon her to the mats of the floor. He went to the ground and inside her so hard that she grunted with the force of it. It had been a long time since he felt a woman under him, and he moved on her with a frantic passion she encouraged and returned. The only resistance came when he tried to pull her gown the rest of the way from her body, but she turned over beneath him and allowed him then, arching her bare back to his chest as he clutched hungrily at hers. His movements behind her kept a pace with the distant *mudhif* drums and with his eyes closed it was like he was there again, the music loud around him as they bucked against each other like animals. He leaned over to smother her throat with hungry bites, and she turned her head so her mouth could find his, and their kisses were filled with their noises while the drums beat. He grabbed and he groped, enjoying one of her breasts then the other, and another, then another, two full rows of them heavy and swaying under her, and with the feeling of that finally registering it seemed her mouth, or his, was suddenly filled with teeth, large teeth, too big, and he broke away with a frightened squeal as he finished inside her.

He pushed himself back from her body and slapped a hand to his mouth, probing for whatever he'd felt there. For a moment, instead of a woman sprawled on the floor before him there was a boar, its back thick with bristly hair, and Owens cried out a second time, turning from the sight to kick and crawl away across the ground.

When he looked back, the imagined boar was gone, and the woman sitting where it had been was raising her discarded garment to dress again. She had two breasts. There was a fresh scar just above and between them, puckered and pale against her dark skin, but then the gown dropped down over her body and he looked at her face.

"Strong, brave warrior," she said.

Owens yanked at his clothes, hurrying to dress himself, to get away, and she laughed.

"Just a man with a rifle," she said.

He fled.

He ran to *mudhif* to warn the others, holding his breath against whatever poison fumes had filled the room, but he was too late.

Several men were enjoying the women as Owens had done. He saw naked bodies bristling with thick hair and open mouths distended with the wicked curves of tusks, faces distorted into snouts and beady eyes gleaming in the lamplight. Around them their companions watched and laughed and encouraged the coupling, reaching to squeeze at nearby teats or stroke at where there was hair. Some of the men grunted like they were pigs themselves, and Owens saw Radhawi take another man's knife to hold with his own at either side of his mouth, mimicking what he saw before him with curved blade tusks. Then he lowered his face to the lap of an amused friend beside him and opened the man's stomach with a violent shake of his head.

Owens clutched at his own as if it had been him, but the others only laughed or ignored it altogether. Even the man attacked merely looked down at where Radhawi nuzzled him open, and when the wound was wide enough he reached inside to disembowel himself while Radhawi moved on to eviscerate another.

More men took up blades and those not rutting were cutting instead, each other and themselves, just as he thought the man on the *tuhul* had done. They made troughs of their bodies and the women fell to feeding with glee, goring for more in an orgy of wilful bloodletting. They snuffled in the cavities of men.

One of the women looked up from the swill her face had been in and saw Owens. She wiped blood from her chin with a hand close to cloven and said, "*Filhu.*"

Stop and feed.

He wanted to tell her no, but his mouth was full of tusks and he was hungry.

BAD DOG

Johnny Mains

IT HAD BEEN one of those walks that suddenly went off in a different direction. We had walked down to Effingham cemetery, but there was a funeral taking place and I thought it would be best not to take the dog in there after the last time; Biscuit breaking free of his lead and starting to hump the leg of one of the pallbearers as he was trying to carry the coffin. It was awful; try as I might I could not disengage Biscuit from the man's leg, the coffin started to wobble dangerously, there was hysterical crying coming from the wife of the deceased and shouts of disapproval from the gathered congregation. It was a complete and utter horrorshow. When I finally managed to get Biscuit free and back on the lead, he trotted next to me, his tongue lolling out of his head, grinning like a loon. He was more than a little pleased with himself.

So, instead we turned left, down into Stour Woods, over the little bridge with the bunch of dead flowers Gorilla-taped to it, stopping briefly so Biscuit could have a drink and take a piss on some wild garlic, and a few minutes later we were into the meat of the walk. It was only then I let Biscuit off the lead and off he went, darting into the undergrowth, under branches, splashing into the river. I was on my phone, scrolling through Facebook, but I'd look up every now and again to see if he was alright. If he went off too far in the distance I'd whistle and he'd come back, but not too close because there was no way he'd want to go back on the lead until he was finished, thank you very much.

I pulled out the doggy bags when he stopped to squat, looking at me as he always did as he shat. I smiled, as I always did, thinking it funny how we project feelings like shame onto our animals. Biscuit clearly didn't give a shit who watched him take a dump.

After he was finished I bent down to pick it up, warm through the impossibly thin plastic of the doggy bag. I prayed that it wouldn't tear; it wouldn't be the first time. The wind blew the stink and I caught a breath of it and started to retch. Biscuit just stared at me. I tied off the bag and walked to a bin and launched it in. As I did, another dog came up to Biscuit, younger, a bouncy labrador who jumped on him and made shrill, happy yipping noises. Biscuit was having none of it and told him off, one sharp snap at his muzzle, one fang raking it. The puppy skittered off back to the safety of his owner, a woman in her thirties—caked-on make-up and a blurriness to the eyes that told me she was either hungover or unsuited to morning living.

"That dog of yours needs to be on a fucking lead!" she shouted at me.

"Your dog started it. My dog simply finished it."

I walked past her and she gave me a look that was pure filth. Biscuit trotted ahead of me and a few seconds later we were around the corner and the woman and her puppy were away, but I could still hear her calling my dog a fucking bastard and that it needed to be destroyed.

We both ducked under a blow-down tree and he was off again, up a hill and wouldn't come back down, no matter how many times I called him. Swearing, I made my way up, the small of my back biting in pain.

"You absolute bugger," I told him off when I reached him. "What the hell are you doing all the way up here?"

I looked around me; I had to admit, the view was rather remarkable – on the other side of the hill, Effingham spread out below. I could see the spire of the church, and beyond that the other woods, Hillary Woods, which continued all the way to Haven, five miles away.

"Well, thank you for this, even though you've half-killed me, it is a remarkable sight." I took my phone out of my pocket, snapped a few pictures and uploaded the best one onto Facebook, Twitter and Instagram.

Biscuit sat by a mound in the earth and lay down by it. I took his lead and sat down next to him, rubbing his head. The notifications on my phone started to ping as people liked the photo across all three platforms. I took another picture of Biscuit as he lay there, his eyes closed, and uploaded that too. Before long there were comments from friends that just proclaimed "BISCUIT!!" – and I smiled and felt lucky that I had such a brilliant and loyal pet.

It started to rain as we walked home and Biscuit gave me THE LOOK which I interpreted as "didn't you check the weather forecast before we came out, you absolute donkey?"

"Sorry, buddy, I didn't. But wait till we get home and I'll give you a turn with the hair dryer and a nice treat, what do you think about that?" He wagged his tail at me.

I half-expected the angry woman to still be hanging around waiting for us, but she and her dog seemed long gone and we walked up the long, meandering hill till we reached our road, Birnam Crescent.

There were two police cars and a dog van parked on the street next to my house.

"I wonder what the neighbour has been up to this time?" I said to myself. Biscuit stopped dead and wouldn't move.

"What's up? What did you do *this* time? Late night partying? Drug dealing?" I picked him up and carried him in my arms. He started to whine gently.

I got to the gate of my house and opened it. Then the police started to get out of their car. A plain clothes and four officers. My blood ran to ice. Had someone died? But why send so many? And unless they were getting me for streaming free porn I was in the clear, the most out-there title on the hard drive was *We All Scream For Ass Cream: Volume 3*.

"Mr Dennis Woodhouse?"

"Yes?"

"I'm Detective Inspector Elspeth Sands, is it okay if we come in?"

"Concerning?"

She looks embarrassed for a second, glances at the floor.

"It's concerning your dog."

"About what happened in the woods just now? The woman phoned you because of that? I don—"

"No. Can we come in please?"

"Okay."

Biscuit continued to whine. I opened the front door, unclipped his lead, and he tore off up the stairs. All four followed me in. I walked into the living-room and confronted them.

"What the hell is going on?"

"There's no other way to say this—but can you give an account of your dog's whereabouts on the 15th July 2017, the 3rd of April to the 18th April 2018 and the 3rd of October to the 20th November 2019?"

"He was with me and my wife for the first date. My wife was dead by the second date, brain tumour, but the dog was with me. He's *my* dog."

"We understand that he would be with you when you were awake, but what about at night, when you were asleep?"

"In his dog basket, at the bottom of the bed."

"We don't believe that to be the case."

DI Sands reached into her bag and pulled out a yellow file, From it she pulled out several photographs and handed them to me.

"What the fuck?" They were of several women, all dead, all in various states of undress. All had been wounded several times. Deep rips in their flesh.

"These women were all mauled to death by an animal. After further forensic inspection that animal was revealed to be a dog. We put the teeth marks through the national canine computer, as you know the law that was brought in at the start of the year that states that all dogs had to have a cast taken of their teeth, otherwise they have to be destroyed?"

"Yes, I took him and got him done. But I don't see . . ."

"Your dog, Mr Woodhouse, his teeth have been found on the remains of eight bodies, one mark deep into bone. We know it wasn't you because we've checked your activity on these occasions – we've gone into your Facebook, phone records and nothing indicates that you've left the house at all apart from your walks in the morning. By all accounts you lead a very lonely existence. But your dog . . ."

"This is mental! Absurd! Do you realise what you're saying?"

"I know how it looks."

All of the officers looked disturbed at this strange turn of events, but said nothing. They were clearly scared of her.

"No, I don't think you fucking do. You're saying that my *dog* somehow has the capacity to think, act and react like a *human being* and when it comes down to the nitty gritty, kill all of these women in the most horrendous ways imaginable, then reverts back to being a dog with those doggy impulses and gives them a few bites on the arse. That he could get my keys, unlock the door to my house, travel how far, how far is the furthest site?"

"Sixty-five miles."

"Are you *listening* to yourself?" I shouted.

DI Sands turned a deep red.

I had had enough. "Just get out of my house."

"Not without the dog."

"Do you have a warrant?"

"No."

"What are you going to use then?"

"The Dangerous Dogs Act."

"You've got to be fucking kidding me."

I pulled out my phone and went onto google and typed in 'Dangerous Dogs Act' and flicked through it.

"Did you bring the disclaimer with you?"

"We did."

"I'm not signing it. It says here you'll need a court order to destroy the dog. Do you have one?"

"No. We want to ask him questions."

"*What?*" My voice was near-breaking. I was

in the *Twilight Zone*. That must be it. I had gone insane.

"We have a firm reason to believe that your dog can also speak fluent English and holds complete conversations with humans."

I passed DI Sands and looked hard at the other officers who were acting very sheepish about the whole, sorry affair. I walked slowly but surely up the stairs and into the office, where I found Biscuit in his usual place, in his bed in the nook under my desk.

"Hey boy," I whispered, rubbing his head. He looked up at me dolefully, his large brown eyes breaking my heart. I scratched his white and brown ears. His tail thumped hard against the side panel of the nook. *Thwump, thwump.*

"I'll protect you," I said, more forcefully this time.

"Thanks," Biscuit said in a strange, almost human voice with a Suffolk accent.

I fell back and landed on the floor with a thump.

I had imagined it, that was all. Biscuit smiled, his tongue hanging out of his mouth, panting like he always did.

I imagined it. DI Sands had brought insanity into the house and it was clearly catching.

I opened my phone and brought up Facebook Live, walked down the stairs and burst into the livingroom through the melee of officers.

"This is DI Sands, she is here to arrest my dog Biscuit, because she thinks *he* is a serial killer! That he has left the house without me knowing, travelled countless miles, kidnapped women and killed them! She's shown me horrible, traumatic photos of the poor victims and is blaming it all on my dog! Everyone knows how much of a comfort he has been since the death of Michelle and now the police want to take him away and *destroy* him!"

"What? No, you can't do that," Sands remonstrated, trying to grab the phone.

"Best, or *worst* of all!" I yell, "they're saying that he can talk! That *a dog* can speak in a human tongue!"

The views started racking up, within a minute it had jumped to 500 viewers.

"So DI Sands, would you like to tell the viewers what it was that made you think my dog had killed someone? It was that he had bitten their buttocks? And that was it? That was the grand sum total of your evidence?" 3,000 viewers.

Sands looked as if she was going to murder me, she shooed the officers away and they all filed out of the house.

"We'll be back Mr Woodhouse, this time with an order to destroy your dog."

"Did you hear that? She wants my dog destroyed because she thinks he's a serial killer of *humans*! Get the fuck out of my house! This'll be going on instagram, and youtube as well you know, you'll be the biggest laughing stock in the whole country Detective Inspector Sands!" 50,000 viewers.

I stood outside my house as the cars pulled out and drove away. I received a last, pure filthy look from Sands.

"Can you believe it?" I said as I turned the camera around and looked at it. "Did I swallow the wrong pill? Is there a glitch in *The Matrix*? Anyway, do your job, internet, send this viral." 68,000 viewers.

The internet did its thing. I turned off the notifications after a few hours as it went mental. Journalists found my phone number, how, I don't know, but they started calling me, asking me for further clarification. Luckily, Sands had dropped the Dangerous Dogs Act disclaimer with Biscuit's name filled out, my name filled out, as owner. Before I turned off my phone I took a photo of that, redacted the more personal information, uploaded it across all of my accounts and switched off the phone. I went upstairs to the office and sat with Biscuit who was fast asleep and cuddled him. After a while it was time for dinner so I went downstairs and he padded behind me and went back to sleep on his bed underneath the front window.

I cooked three chicken breasts, two for me and one for Biscuit. I microwaved some rice, mixed in some mayonnaise and chopped his portion up into little chunks, put all of it into his bowl and placed it down on the floor. As soon as he heard the clink he came through, at his own pace, but interested, sniffing the air.

I microwaved a separate bag of brown rice and a cup of frozen peas with a bit of water in the bottom of the cup at the same time, then I burst into tears. It took a while for me to calm down. When I did and opened the microwave, I had completely lost my appetite, so I chopped up my meal and dumped it in his bowl with the rice and peas.

"There you go, you lucky bugger," I smiled at him. He was at my feet, he always was. Twelve years I had had him, through thick and thin. We doted on each other and to think that some jumped up police fucker could storm into my house and threaten to take him away made my blood boil. Biscuit started to eat and I walked through to the living room, to the cabinet by the garden-facing window, and took out a photo album that had the very first pictures of him that me and Michelle took when we first got him from the dog's home. Michelle, her long ginger hair on Biscuit's little puppy head. He was smiling, his tongue lolling out. His forever home.

I flicked through the photos, smiling until I came to the selfie of me and Biscuit that I took on the day of Michelle's funeral. He came with me that day, of course he did. He didn't stop whining when I came in and told him that she had died. He lay by her coffin in the church and broke everyone's heart. I plugged the landline into the wall and rang Michelle's mum. Sheila picked up on the third ring.

"You're all over the news, you know. Do you think you should have embarrassed her like that? It's the end of her career, they're saying."

"I know," I sighed. "But I *really* felt as if I was in an episode of *The Twilight Zone,* and if I didn't record it then say something afterwards, nobody would have believed me. And if she's that unfit for her job then it's clear that she shouldn't be in it. I've turned everything off, what are they saying about her?"

"She is . . . was . . . a hotshot detective who single-handedly solved that serial killer case in Etchnard. She was kidnapped and managed to escape."

"The killer daughter that worked with her dad? She was *that* detective? Holy hell!"

Shelia didn't say anything as I digested the news.

"It's a big scalp. And I don't think this'll go away for a while. As soon as you hang up, pull the phone out of the socket again, and make sure there's no journalists hiding in any of the neighbour's houses when you go let Biscuit out into the garden when he needs the toilet."

"I was just about to do that just now, thanks for the heads up."

"Her third anniversary on Tuesday," Sheila said quietly.

"I know." I didn't want to say any more, because both of us would start to cry.

"I'll phone you then. I'm going up the loft on Monday, having a sort out, might find some of her University stuff that you've not seen before."

"That would be really lovely, some of her artwork that she was always talking about but never wanted to show me for some reason."

"Well, it wasn't *that* good." A pause. Then we both broke into laughter.

After our goodbyes I hung up the phone and went out of the house, into the back garden, and walked up to the massive bay tree with the emanuelle chair hanging from it. Michelle's chair.

I sat in it, the branch squeaking with alarm as my full weight went into it.

Biscuit padded out about five minutes later and sat at my feet, looking up at me, expectantly.

His eyes worked their magic.

"A walk? Okay then, you mischievous bugger. Let's go into the woods then, shall we?"

We both went indoors. I grabbed his lead and clipped it onto his collar, and I purposefully left my mobile in the kitchen as I didn't want to be bothered by anyone. I poked my head out of the house, the street was uncharacteristically empty. I sighed, opened up the boot and Biscuit jumped in.

I drove off wondering if I'd be followed by at least one or two journos with nothing else on their hands to do.

I parked the car up at Hillary Woods and opened up the boot. Biscuit jumped out nimbly. His tail wagged hard as I unclipped his lead, and he scampered off into the woods. The trees that heavy wet smell to them and for a moment, a brief moment, I felt happier than I had for a while.

I walked up a small hill and when I got to the top I saw Biscuit, low, growling at someone in front of him. Someone wearing a hood, obscuring their features.

I ran down to him, and as I got closer, saw that the figure was holding a knife.

"Get away from my dog," I yelled.

"Your dog is a *fucking* killer and it's destroyed my *fucking* life." The person pulled back their hooded top. It was DI Elspeth Sands. Her face was white with rage, her eyes wide and furious, never leaving the dog's.

"Biscuit, come here," I commanded. Biscuit ignored me, he was as zeroed in on Sands as she was on him.

"Look, I'm aware of the stresses you've been under with your work—" I started.

"Your dog is a serial killer. That's all there is to it. And I'm going to put him down so he can't kill anyone else."

"Right, that's it, I've had enough. I'm calling the police." Then I realised I had left my phone back at the house. I tried to change tact. "Elspeth, do you realize how *insane* this all sounds? Serial killing dogs, being able to speak English—"

"Well, not all *that* insane, Dennis." A new

voice had entered the conversation.

Elspeth retched and fell back, staggered onto the ground. She started to scream.

"*See? See? I told you, I fucking* knew *it.*" The hysteria in her voice could have shattered glass. She scrambled away and took off, leaving behind the knife.

My brain seemed to drop a hundred thousand feet and splat onto a very hard surface.

"Don't worry Dennis, I won't kill you. You're my master. But that bitch—" Biscuit said in his rather broad Suffolk accent, as he brought himself up onto his two back paws, his body cracking, re-shaping and forming as he became human-like in his physicality, "—is so fucked."

Biscuit bent down and picked up the knife with his hand-like paw—and it was weird to see how his legs bent inwards as he did it—and then he took off after Elspeth very, very fast.

A minute later I heard the screams and they were loud and wet and awful until they were rapidly cut off.

Biscuit padded back after the job was done, and he was back in his doggy form. He was smiling but breathing hard, his tongue lolling out of his mouth.

"Right, Dennis," he huffed, as he stood by me and waited for me to clip the lead back on him, "when we get home we're going to have to have a long chat about things and—"

"Elspeth. They're going to come straight to my house," I said, my whole body gripped with panic.

"Nope they're not, when they find her they'll think she's sliced her own throat. Honestly mate, you're fine. Totally in the clear. Just run me through a puddle to get this blood off my paws.

Actually, come to think of it, what I *would* do, though, is smooth out that area over there where she dropped to the ground, that *might* make someone suspicious"

We walked back to the car in silence and I opened up the boot and Biscuit hopped in, as neat as you please.

"On the way home, can you pull into the chip shop and buy me some fish? I've missed my fish. Michelle used to buy me it all the time."

I closed the boot on Biscuit and drove home, fighting the urge to crash the car into a tree at a hundred miles an hour.

Elspeth's death was regarded as suicide, the Coroner decided, brought on by the severe trauma of her kidnapping. Biscuit and I have come to an understanding—I continue to feed and fuss him, and he won't kill me 'in the most gruesome way imaginable.' He's told me everything, as much as he is able, about how he got to where he is today. The revelation that my wife *knew* about who Biscuit really was and that they were having an affair has made me sick to my core. Is he making it up to get at me or to destroy all that I am?

"Go and get me some dinner, there's a good boy," he says, from the comfort of his doggie bed by the television.

His tail goes *thwump, thwump* as I make my way to the kitchen.

THE CULL

Kit Power

"NO, THE WINE! Grab the fucking wine, you idiot!"

Jason felt himself beginning to blush as he walked back towards Tara, the heat running up his cheeks, making his scalp tingle. He hated it. Hated his trembling hands, his unsteady step as he not-quite-ran back to join her at the entrance to the village hall.

"What the fuck is this, Jason?"

He held up the packets of After Eights sheepishly, cursing himself for what he realised was a deeply childish decision. He'd panicked, he supposed; stood in front of the prize hamper, paralyzed by the sheer volume of desirable items, when he saw the wafer-thin mints, his mind flashed to happy memories of the Christmas holidays, the only time he'd normally eat them, and his hands had made the call for him.

"They're really nice," he said, hating the defensive whine in his voice.

"You knobhead," said Tara, smiling, and Jason felt his blush deepen. From inside the hall, the National Farmers Union youth wing (North Devon branch) Christmas party roared with laughter at something. From where they stood outside the hall, all Jason could hear of the entertainment was a series of deep booms from an amplified male voice.

Tara rolled her eyes. "I'll sort it out."

She started to walk back into the hall, towards the wicker basket, overflowing with goodies, that sat on the table in the antechamber. Jason grabbed her arm, and hissed "wait!", but she shrugged him off and strode over to the table, her long green army jacket flapping behind her. *She looks like a goddamn gunslinger,* thought Jason, and he felt a familiar surge of love, so strong it made him feel a little ill. The fucking guts of it; of *her.*

Jason stared at the door into the main hall, willing it to stay shut. Just 30 more seconds. Just that. She reached out and grasped the neck of the bottle of white wine, and Jason once more cursed his own stupidity; why hadn't he just done that in the first place? In one fluid moment, Tara lifted the bottle from the hamper and swept it inside her jacket, turning towards Jason, a smile already rising on her face. Jason began to smile back.

Two things happened in quick succession. The first was that a clingfilm wrapped fruitcake, displaced by the removal of the wine bottle, hit the floor with an audible splat, rolling a couple of feet towards Jason before settling.

The second was the door to the main hall started to open.

The surge of adrenaline was so intense that Jason actually leapt into the air; he felt the impact in his feet as they connected back with the ground. He caught sight of a thick looking arm inside a flannel shirt, fat pink fingers gripping the door handle, and then, with a shriek of "Run!" —he turned and fled. He thought he heard Tara behind him, but he didn't look back, focussing on building momentum, making distance. He heard a deep male voice yell out "Hey!" and put on a further spurt of speed, running full pelt down the side of the building, towards the wooden fence that marked the edge of the common land the

Village Hall was built on. The loose gravel crunched under his Doc Martins, scattering a spray of small stones behind him as his legs pumped. Sure he could hear someone close in pursuit, he leapt at the fence, vaulting it with a speed and agility that, under other circumstances, he might have celebrated. As it was, he ran on into the sudden darkness of the meadow, the cold winter air wrapping around him. The field was on a steep downward slope, and soon the light from the hall and car park behind him was cut off by the brow of the hill.

A couple of seconds after that, his heel hit something slippery, and his legs pinwheeled out from under him. He hit the ground hard, knocking the air from his lungs and bouncing the back of his skull off the cold turf hard enough to hurt. He sat up, rubbing the back of his head gingerly, straining his ears for the sound of pursuit.

He heard nothing.

No, wait . . . there *was* something. But it was coming from further down the hill. *Sheep?* He'd seen them grazing in the field before, and, as his nose finally caught up with his new situation, he realised with dismay that he was lying in, and had likely slipped in, some fresh droppings. His face wrinkled in disgust.

Where's Tara?

The thought stabbed at him. She'd been right behind him, surely, he'd heard someone else running, it had to be her, *had* to . . .

So where is she, then?

He cursed under his breath, and got up on one knee, peering up the hill, towards the light, hoping he'd see her silhouette as she reached the brow of the hill. He thought about calling her name but decided it would be a bad idea. If someone was chasing her . . .

Or if they've already got her . . .

The thought made him feel dizzy, sick with shame. He'd just run, left her. He should go back. He couldn't go back. He couldn't . . .

What is that noise?

It didn't sound like sheep. It was a shuffling, grunting noise. And it was coming from all around him, it seemed like.

And it was getting closer.

Jason reached into his jacket pocket with hands that were not quite steady, and pulled out his battered Harley Davidson Zippo lighter, gripping it tight. The metallic pinging noise as he flipped it open sounded painfully loud to him, but he didn't hesitate, spinning the wheel with his thumb.

On the second attempt, the wick sprung into flame.

Jason sat, momentarily frozen in place.

A thousand points of light shone at him. Ten thousand. A blanket of stars, low to the ground, an ocean wave of lights, undulating, rippling towards him. *Eyes,* his mind told him, blankly, but Jason couldn't process the thought, what the thought must mean; instead, his ears soaked up the grunting, shuffling noise that grew louder as the wave of lights closed in. He stood, holding up the lighter, turning his head, all thoughts of pursuers gone like smoke in the breeze, turning his head from side to side. The lights were pouring in from all directions, rushing up the hill. As he watched, he heard a crashing, tearing sound, and suddenly a line of darkness that he realised had been a hedgerow collapsed, revealing another sea of tiny stars *(eyes)*, gleaming in the reflected flame.

They were moving so fast that the front wave was almost upon him before the flame revealed the creatures behind the eyes. Jason screamed then, a high pitched squeal of terror that shredded his throat, leaving him with the taste of blood. Then blind panic set in, and he turned and flung himself back up the hill, towards the village hall.

Tara was trying not to panic.

Easier said than done. She was in pain, for one thing; as she'd started to run after Jason, her third step had come down hard on the fruitcake, and the resulting slimy mush had sent her flying, landing on her tailbone hard enough to make her yelp and clicking her teeth together, drawing blood from the side of her tongue. To add insult to injury, she'd also dropped the wine bottle, and the bottom of her jeans were now soaked, stinking, and clung uncomfortably to her legs.

Then there was the small matter of the half nelson she was currently being held in.

The man was a local farmer. She'd seen him about the village, at the Post Office, and driving about in his mud-spattered Range Rover. She'd never seen him absent his flat cap, waxed green full-length raincoat and corduroy trousers, and the thick glasses and full moustache on a chubby face had always made him seem a somewhat comical figure.

His grip around her wrist was strong. Painful. Up close, he smelt of animal dung and sweat. She didn't find him funny anymore. Not one bit. Her skin crawled.

"Thief, is it? Well, well, now. Tara Jenkins. Scum of the earth." She could hear the smile in his voice, feel his hot breath on the back of her neck. She fought to stay calm.

"And who was that, running off? Your boyfriend, Jason Everington, I'd wager?"

"He's not my boyfriend!" The words were out immediately; a bone-deep instinctive response to falsehood she couldn't control.

The man behind her laughed, and tightened his already painful grip. "Oh, I don't care if he's slipping you one or not - between you and I, he strikes me as one of those bum boys, most likely. What matters is I've finally caught the pair of you at something you can pay for."

Tara let off a stream of very colourful swearwords, in the privacy of her own skull. She and Jason had been the bane of the local fox hunt since the new season opened in October; a sympathetic farmer's daughter they knew from school had leaked to them the time and location of the village hunt starting locations, and Jason and Tara had put their meagre pocket money to good use, buying up bags of aniseed balls from the bemused village shopkeeper, and sewing the field with the sweets late the night before. The first time they'd pulled the stunt, they'd hidden in a nearby copse of trees the following morning, delighting in the moment the hounds were released only to scatter across the entire field, hunting down the sweets and completely ignoring any fox scents there may have been.

Realising it had been an unnecessary risk, they'd not watched subsequent hunt meets, but their source on the inside delighted in feeding them locations and reporting back the increasing fury of her father and his friends. And the village hunt had, by December, become the laughing stock of the entire North Devon region - enough that the NFU had talked about relocating their youth Christmas party elsewhere. In the end, a paucity of suitable venues and a non-refundable deposit had ensured the event went ahead, albeit with some bad feeling.

Tara was feeling pretty bad about it herself, just at that moment.

"Let me go!" She was proud of how her voice sounded; strong, indignant, and not a bit scared. The anger was keeping the panic at bay, and that was good, too.

The man laughed, and she felt a fine spray of saliva on the back of her neck. "You ain't going nowhere, missy. I may not be able to prove you and your *boyfriend* had anything to do with our dismal hunting season, but I'm certainly going to press full charges over this little escapade. We'll see how clever you feel with a criminal record."

Tara tried to think it through, process the claim rationally, ignore the threat. She was fourteen years old. Had never been in any prior trouble with the law. Sure, she'd been caught red-handed, but . . . "They're not going to do anything to me, I'm just a kid! If you hurt my arm, though—"

She felt the pressure on her arm momentarily tighten, and gritted her teeth against the pain, but then it loosened. She heard the man behind her grunt with disappointment. "I'm not hurting you, just making sure you don't run. Citizen's arrest."

"Well, if you're going to call the police, call them! We'll see what they have to say about you trying to break a girl's arm!"

The grip on her wrist loosened further.

"I'm not trying to break your arm! Serve you bloody right if I did though, you and that queer boy you run with. Scum, the pair of you. Trying to wreck our way of life with your tree-hugging nonsense. Fucking disgrace."

"Oh, yeah, the noble tradition of chasing an innocent animal on horseback before having it ripped apart by hounds. Scum? Look in the mirror!"

He leaned closer, hissing in her ear. His breath stank of fruit-flavoured chewing gum.

"It's pest control! Foxes are vermin! Get them in a coup, they'll kill everything that flaps. We have to keep them under control."

"Yeah, I can tell you're big on control."

"You watch your mouth! You're in enough trouble!" He was almost shouting now, but he was barely holding her wrist at all. Laura forced herself to stay calm. She might yet be able to get out of this, if she could get lucky and keep him distracted.

"Why don't you just admit that you enjoy murdering innocent creatures?"

"You don't understand a thing, little miss. It's for the greater good. Foxes kill chickens. Badgers spread disease, they have to be kept under control . . ."

"Badgers? Who said anything about badgers?" Tara felt her heart rate pick up, unease in her stomach.

"Yup. Had the cull just this afternoon. The set over near the moor. Had to. They spread TB, sure enough, and we can't afford another loss of cattle—"

Tara felt tears threatening, suddenly. The set he was talking about was huge, many hundreds of animals . . . "That's protected! You can't—"

His chuckle chilled her to the bone. "Got the order overturned in the morning, job was done by the afternoon. Don't worry, missy, we were very humane. And think of all the cows we've saved. Now, I'm just going to make a phone call to the local station over in Torrington. One of the Supers over there is a friend. I'm sure he'll—"

A distant piercing scream cut the man off mid-sentence. Tara felt a stab of fear send energy surging through her system, and as the man's grip momentarily loosened further, she put the energy into action. She dug the heel of her right boot into the man's upper calf, and dragged it down his instep as hard as she could, stomping down on his ankle bone. He howled with pain, and she twisted her wrist; the motion, aided by the man's sweaty hands, broke his grip. Driving her free elbow back as hard as she could, she felt a solid impact, and heard a satisfying *oof* noise; then she was running, straight arm slamming the door open.

She ran the same path Jason had taken, along the edge of the hall, straight at the fence that led to the dark field beyond. She felt confident that the farmer wouldn't pursue her very far in the darkness; of course, the sadistic bastard would still call the cops, and she and Jason would need to figure out what they were going to say, but that was a problem for later, and that suited Tara just fine.

She was perhaps twenty feet from the fence when she skidded to a halt, eyes wide, mouth sprung open.

Jason was running toward her. He was pale, almost translucent, that pathetic ginger goatee he'd spent the last six months trying to cultivate hanging from his bone-white chin like the world's crappest caterpillar. His arms and legs were pumping frantically, and his face showed nothing but blind terror.

Then Tara heard the noise, and looked at the ground behind him.

For a couple of precious seconds, what she saw defied her reason. All she could make out was an undulating sea of black and white, a tidal wave perhaps a foot high, accompanied by a series of overlapping snuffling grunts and the crunch of frozen grass being trampled. As she watched, the tide closed on Jason, still several strides from the fence. It reached his ankle, and suddenly distinct forms burst from the morass, the creatures climbing his legs. Jason pitched forward immediately, giving out a single strangled cry. Several of the badgers closed on him, and Tara saw claws shredding cloth with a wet ripping sound, exposing raw, bloody flesh. Within a couple of seconds, there was merely a Jason shaped lump on the field, completely covered in black and white fur. From under the seething shape, she heard scraping, snapping sounds, and saw splashes of red, but Jason said no more.

The rest of the tide was still coming.

As it reached the fence, her paralysis broke, and she turned and ran.

As she did so, she saw the man who had been holding her, about halfway down the side of the building. She saw his eyes widen comically with surprise at her sudden change of direction, but she had no time to enjoy the moment; instead, mind and body moving together with the liquid speed gifted by terror and adrenaline, she headed straight for him, janking right at the last moment and slamming him off balance with her shoulder. She staggered from the impact, but held her feet and picked her speed back up, ignoring his startled cry.

As she reached the corner of the building and turned to run back inside, she heard him cry out again. Then he screamed.

She didn't look back.

She pulled the front door open hard enough that it bounced back on its hinges as she darted into the entranceway, then slammed open the double doors into the main hall.

She took in the scene with one sweep of her head. The hall she knew well, from years of youth clubs, school plays, and bring and buy sales; a polished wooden floor that ran the length of the rectangular building, a series of large glass windows on the long opposite wall, with a stage at the far end, and a fire door at the near. A crowd of teenagers, perhaps fifty or sixty, were in the process of clearing the floor, stacking the chairs that had been laid in rows in front of the stage neatly against the wall. On the stage, she recognised the light show rig from one of the mobile discos that sometimes played in town. Ignoring the fact that all activity had ground to a halt, and that several dozen people were now staring at her with varying degrees of curiosity and hostility, she looked up.

The ceiling was high and arched, with crossbeams running between the sloped section of the roof; like a loft space without the boards. Would it be high enough? She thought so; she remembered reading that badgers could climb, but couldn't jump. Of course, these badgers were hardly normal, but maybe—

She looked back at the stage, and felt a surge of hope. In the far corner, a huge Christmas tree stood, the top rising far past the crossbeams Tara wanted to reach, a ridiculous yellow star glittering down at her.

Merry fucking Christmas, she thought, the screams of the farmer still ringing in her ears.

"Excuse me, um, but this is a private party?" The voice managed to sound both apologetic and angry at the same time. Tara focussed on the source; a blonde, tousle-haired teenager in a thin, open-necked shirt that showed rather too much of his pink hairless chest for Tara's taste.

"Not for long," she replied, loudly, pointing at the window.

The boy turned to look, and so did everyone else.

Everyone except Tara.

Tara ran.

She wove between the suddenly stationary chair stackers, making the straightest line she could for the stage. She took the two-foot edge in a single step, dove around the edge of the DJ rig, and ran for the tree.

Behind her, she heard the sound of shattering glass, followed immediately by screams; first of fear, then pain.

Up close, the tree wasn't quite as sturdy as it had seemed from a distance. The trunk looked thick enough, she thought, but the branches seemed perilously thin. Experimentally, she reached up and grabbed one, pulling as hard as she could. It snapped off in her hand.

Behind her, the screams grew louder, more desperate. The snuffling grunting noise echoed off the walls, along with moist tearing sounds. There was a smell; wet mud and copper.

She grabbed the trunk of the tree as best she could, but the branches around were too thick, making it hard to get a grip. She tried pulling herself up, swinging her legs around either side, hoping to climb it the way she did the fireman's pole back in the park, but the density of the thin limbs prevented her from getting a proper grip, and she couldn't move up the tree. Worse, she felt the whole thing wobbling under her weight, and she realised if she persisted, it was likely to tip over.

Fuck.

The panic that adrenaline and action had so far kept at bay started to claw at her mind. She spun around, frantic, head moving in all directions. Looking for a way up.

She looked at the DJ booth.

The bank of lights stood near the edge of the stage, six rectangular blocks with the decks behind the centre two, at roughly her shoulder height. She looked up from there at the rafters. Did the stage plus the light blocks give her enough extra height to reach them?

She thought maybe.

In any case, the frantic shouts and pained screams from the hall told her she was out of options, and running out of time.

Two steps took her to the nearest box, and she jumped, placing her palms flat on the top and pushing herself up. Quickly, she got a knee underneath her, then raised to a standing position. The top was narrow enough that she had to place her feet angled sideways for balance, and she felt sure the thing would tip at any moment, sending her plunging into the carnage below. She kept her eyes fixed up, ignoring the kinetic movement and flashes of black, white and red from her peripheral vision. The nearest rafter was almost close enough for the tips of her fingers to reach . . . if she leant forward, which struck her as a supremely dumb idea. But it was close enough, she thought.

If she timed the jump right.

She crouched down, taking a deep breath. Really, it wasn't so tough; she'd made more daring leaps on the climbing frame at the village green. *You can do this. You can.*

Do it. Now!

As her legs started to straighten, and she took the leap, she felt the light stand sway under her, as though something had collided with it. There was a sickening lurch, and her stomach dropped as her jumping-off point tipped away from under her feet. She was still in the air, still rising, but she'd lost precious power, and as a result, the beam was not where she'd expected it to be—

GRAB IT! Her mind cried, and her arms flailed, reaching frantically. She hooked the beam with her left arm, and as she swung forward, grabbed her left wrist with her right hand, ignoring the jarring pain in her shoulder as it took her weight. From below, even over the screams and those awful tearing sounds, she heard the crash of the lighting rack falling, a heavy thump accompanied by the almost musical tinkling of broken glass.

Don't look down.

She looked up instead, at the beam that she held in a death grip. Slowly, using her shoulder, back and stomach muscles, she pulled her body parallel with the beam, before swinging her leg over with a grunt of effort. Once positioned, it was easy enough for her to swivel her hips, using the leg and arm, to bring her body on top of the beam.

She lay across it for a couple of breaths, hugging it tightly, eyes screwed shut, allowing herself a moment to take it in. She'd made it. She was safe.

Then she opened her eyes.

The floor of the village hall looked like a slaughterhouse.

Tara watched, breath catching in her throat, as the badgers tore the teenagers apart. Most of the ones who were still alive were bunched up at the front and fire doors. The seething mass of creatures climbed their backs, claws digging into flesh with a wet punching sound, snouts digging into backs, necks, jaws snapping, teeth tearing. She watched, terror granting a merciful detachment, as one after another, the people were dragged to the floor by sheer weight of numbers, where they were torn apart, howling, and crying, sounds that would grow louder, then become bubbly and damp, before ceasing. Through the broken glass of the windows, the badgers were still pouring in, grunting and scrabbling over the sill, then waddling over the backs of the creatures already inside.

Why can't they get out? The voice asking the question was dull and uninterested, and Tara found herself surprised at her capacity for curiosity, however idle. Nevertheless, as the boy in the open-necked shirt, who'd been so rude to her when she'd run in, shrieked in pain as the creatures opened his stomach with their claws and started gnawing at his intestines, she got her answer; the half a dozen people left at the fire escape managed to force the door open a crack, only for more badgers to pour in through the opening.

Tara turned away. The screams told the story well enough. She didn't need to see any more.

Back on the stage, mercifully free of people, the badgers spread out, knocking over the remaining lighting rigs and the DJ's decks. As they swarmed toward the tree, Tara felt a momentary stab of dull, black, resignation – *oh, well, I tried, guess they'll get me anyway* – but as a dozen of the creatures started to scale it, the tree tipped over. Tara saw the star bounce off the top of the tree, coming to rest on top of a bloody blond scalp that two badgers were gnawing at.

Eventually, the feeding stopped.

When it was done, the badgers started doing something else. It took Tara a while to figure out what it was. Once she had, she felt her sanity give way with a simple snapping feeling in her mind. It was a welcome relief.

Superintendent Marks stood just inside the main room of the village hall, staring in disbelief at the floor. Beside him, officer Stephens, who had been first on the scene, shifted from foot to foot.

"One survivor?" Marks spoke, not looking away from the tableau.

"Yes, sir. She's with the ambulance. Not talking so far. Catatonic, they think. She was on that rafter. They had to peel her off it, sir."

"I'll bet. They probably want to make sure she's still got a tongue to speak with."

"Sir?"

"Never mind."

The two men stood, staring at the floor.

"What's that, Stephens?"

"Pretty sure that's a piece of large intestine, sir."

"That's what I thought. And that?"

"Erm, skin?"

"Possibly. And over there?"

"I'm really not sure, sir."

"Me either. But if I had to bet, I'd say they were testicles, removed from the scrotum."

The two men stood in silence for a while.

"How many were supposed to be here?"

Stephens turned to his notebook with relief, grateful to no longer have to stare at the detritus in front of them. "Latest estimate is seventy three, sir. Mostly teenagers, plus the organisers, a couple of volunteers, the DJ . . ."

"There's nothing like seventy three people's worth of remains, here, Stephens."

Stephens didn't reply. Eventually, his eyes returned to the arrangement of human remains on the blood-splattered floor of the hall, and he asked, in a quiet, plaintiff voice, "What do you think it means, sir?"

Superintendent Marks looked at the scattered body parts, bones, and entrails on the floor, their arrangement spelling out the message

LEEV UZ ALOWN

He sighed.

"I think," he said, fishing out a cigarette from a battered packet in his coat pocket, "it means, Christmas is fucking cancelled, Stephens."

He lit up the cigarette, drew the smoke deep into his lungs, and held it there.

RED ANTLERS

Charlotte Bond

IT WAS A particularly fine Friday morning, with a low mist on the ground but a clear blue sky that promised the sun would soon burn away any damp. Ian hummed to himself as he walked the perimeter of the Johnston Hall estate, enjoying the autumn colours while keeping his eyes open for any damage to the wire fence that might suggest one of the deer under his care had escaped. The locals were pretty good at dropping him a text about any escapees, so he wasn't particularly worried by the bent section in the fence close to the eastern gate. What confused him, though, was that the wire was bent inward, as if something had leaped in rather than out.

With no further anomalies uncovered, he found his deer grazing contentedly in one of their usual spots. Nothing seemed to be troubling them, and a head count indicated that they were all there.

He walked away, his mind already running through the upcoming jobs of the day. If he'd looked back, he would have seen the stag emerging from a stand of trees, watching him walk away. He wouldn't have been close enough to see the foam around its mouth, but he couldn't have failed to miss the blood glistening red on its antlers.

Standing next to her Fiesta, Melissa zipped her coat up to the chin. *Why the hell did I move to the North?* she thought. *Sure, it smells in London, and it's noisy. But it's* warm. *What the hell was I thinking?*

What she'd been thinking was just how much cheaper it was to rent a flat in Leeds than it was in London. As her feet crunched on the gravel and her breath misted in the air, she wished she'd thought of other things.

Still, I can always wear more jumpers, she reasoned, *especially as I can afford more clothes than when I lived in Bromley.*

Only the Johnston family were allowed to park in front of the Hall, mainly because their Bentleys contributed to the ambience of the place. Lowly cafe employees like Melissa had to park out near the old stables and then walk a decent way through along a tree-lined avenue to get to work. Melissa didn't mind in the summer, but in autumn the walk was damp and gloomy.

A noise from the trees on her left made her slow then stop altogether, listening. The crunch of gravel behind her made her spin round. There was a stag on the path, staring at her. Normally, sighting a deer on her walk to work would lift her spirits, like glimpsing a bit of nature made manifest. But there was nothing uplifting about this creature. Its huge, muscular body spoke only of intimidation, its stare of dominance.

Okay, okay. Keep calm. Ian said they're only aggressive in the rutting season. Is it rutting season? Shit. Why didn't I pay more attention instead of staring at his eyes.

Well, he definitely said not to run. They'll chase you. Make yourself look big. Don't hunch over. She straightened and stuck out her chest. The deer twitched an ear.

Slowly, Melissa walked backwards, never taking her eyes from the stag. To her dismay, it matched her step for step, not closing the distance but not letting her edge away either. As it passed through a patch of sunlight, Melissa saw that its antlers were stained dark red.

Despite Ian's words, she turned and pelted down the path, gravel kicking up around her. She didn't glance over her shoulder in case she stumbled and fell. She didn't stop running until she'd reached the door of an outbuilding where the path curved round. Only then did she turn to face her pursuer.

The stag was still in the same spot. Idly, it scented the air before wandering back into the trees.

"You little fucker," Melissa muttered. She took a few moments to get her breathing and legs under control before she set off again.

As she walked, she typed a message to Ian.

Hey there. How's things? Haven't seen you in a while. Just saw a deer. It had blood on its antlers. Thought I'd better tell you.

Her finger hovered over the 'x', uncertain whether she should add a kiss to the end. She would for any other friend, but could Ian really be called a friend when she always wished he'd be something more? Even while she was going out with James?

She sent the text as it was and continued on to the cafe.

All of Ian's good humour vanished the moment he received Melissa's text. He cursed himself for not investigating the bent fence more closely. What if one of his bucks was dead? Or lying somewhere in agony?

The sun was up, which meant that the deer would be moving away from their dawn open grazing areas into the shelter of the trees. Ian followed a game trail that would take him past their favourite spots while keeping him down-wind.

After many years of being a deer warden, he moved silently without even thinking about it, avoiding twigs that would snap or water that would squelch. As he walked, his mind went over various explanations.

The blood could be from another deer or maybe a dog that got into the park. There'd been that awful incident two years back with a holidaymaker that couldn't control his spaniel. Ian would get it in the neck if something like that had happened again.

Glancing up from the trail, he stopped dead. There was a stag standing about twelve feet away; it had blood on its antlers and froth around its mouth.

Holy Shit.

Ian stood very still, examining the creature. It was a red deer, but not one of his herd. He could tell each of his fifty-six animals apart, all of them by name according to a unique feature: White Spot, Floppy Ear, Split Ear, and so on. If he'd had to name this deer, it would have been called Mean Looking Bastard.

The stag's ear tag had been ripped out, quite some time ago by the look of the wound. The blood on its antlers was dark, dry, and flaking, which made Ian feel a little better. Whatever injuries it had inflicted had been some time past. If it had been another deer, he would have found it by now; if it had been a dog, the police would already be breathing down his neck.

The stag tossed its head slightly. Ian knew the danger signs to look out for: snorting, bellowing, lowering the head. This creature exhibited none of them but still managed to project an aura of menace.

Still, it was on his land, so it was his problem.

"Hey there," he said softly. "Been in a fight, have we?"

The stag twitched an ear but otherwise didn't move. Ian decided that the best thing to do was quietly retreat then call round his fellow wardens and see if anyone was missing a stag.

They can collect the damn thing themselves, he thought grimly. *No way I'm attempting to get that creature into a trailer.*

"Well, nice to meet you," he said, taking a step backwards. "I'm just going to make a few calls and see if I can get you home."

For every step Ian took, the deer matched him. He swallowed hard.

"Tell you what, I'll just head this way instead," he said, walking to his left, deeper into the trees. Always good to have a tree as a barrier between you and a stag.

The deer started walking parallel to him, a classic threatening manoeuvre; everything about its stance spoke of silent aggression. Ian knew he should identify a tree he could climb if necessary, but he didn't dare take his eyes off the animal.

With deliberate care, he eased the shotgun off his shoulder, pointing at the ground. He'd only brought it thinking that he might need to put an injured animal out of its misery, not defend himself. The deer stopped, its gaze swivelling to the weapon. There was an unnerving intelligence to its bloodshot eye.

For a long minute, man and beast faced each other. Then the deer turned and walked away. Ian counted to fifty before he resumed walking backwards. Only when the stag was lost among the trees did he allow himself to turn his back on it and hurry back to his warden's hut. He repeatedly looked over his shoulder, convinced he'd see the maddened creature charging towards him, but it had vanished.

Melissa's cafe assistant, Betty, was late in that morning, and Melissa had pretty much set out all the cakes and got the savouries in the oven by the time the old woman sauntered through the door. "Oh, Melissa, love, what tales I have to tell you!" Betty exclaimed as she hung up her coat.

Edging close to seventy, Betty was still spry and had the filthiest jokes Melissa had ever heard. While it had been undeniably quieter while Betty was visiting her sister, Melissa had missed the old woman's grin and her flirtation with customers a quarter of her age.

Melissa made them both a cup of tea and they set about folding a new set of napkins and refilling the sugar and sauce bowls while Betty related her sordid stories. Soon, Melissa was chuckling to herself, the incident with the deer quite forgotten.

"And how has young James been?" Betty asked, a twinkle in her eye.

"Oh, you know," Melissa said distractedly. "Fine. Just ambling along. We saw that new James Bond movie."

"Nothing more exciting?" Betty prompted.

Melissa hesitated. Things with James were just as she described them: ambling. Nothing disappointing, but nothing exciting either. But she wasn't quite ready to admit that it might be the beginning of the end, so instead she said, "Well, James has something special planned tonight. He said to meet him by the back entrance."

"Taking you up the back entrance, is he?" Betty snorted; Melissa rolled her eyes.

"You know that's not my kind of thing at all."

"It's not how people think it is, you know, I, myself, am rather fond of— oh! Hello, Ian." Melissa cursed her traitorous heart from lurching as the deer warden came in. She thought she was mostly over her feelings for him, but when he'd stayed late the other day to help her sort a late delivery, Melissa had reflected afterwards that forty-five minutes with Ian had left her smiling more than a whole evening with James.

"Hello both," Ian said, looking flustered. "Can I grab some coffee to go, please?" he asked, holding out his flask.

"Sure," said Betty, taking it. "Had a rough morning?"

"Kinda." He ran his hands anxiously through his hair.

"Did you find that deer?" Melissa asked, piling up the napkins.

"Yeah. I think so. I think it might have escaped from somewhere. It's certainly not one of ours."

"Melissa!" Betty called from the kitchen. "Want to give Ian something hot to hold?"

Melissa and Ian shared an embarrassed grin before she fetched the flask, ignoring Betty's lecherous wink.

"Here you go. Anything else you need?" she asked as she handed over the coffee.

"No, just keep an eye out and if you see the animal again, drop me another text, yeah? Don't go near it. I mean, I'm sure it's fine but—do you remember all the stuff I told you?"

"Oh yes. Don't stare them down. Put something between yourself and the deer. Don't curl into a ball. Don't run. Climb a tree."

He grinned, evidently impressed. "Definitely keep those in mind if you meet this deer again. He's a big bastard. Even *I* was a little intimidated."

"I can't imagine that," she said, flashing him a charming smile before she could stop herself.

To her dismay, he looked a little awkward. But then he surprised her by saying, "Are you doing anything tonight? Only you were interested in which deer was which, and I've got to pull together some named photos for a display so I thought you could come to the hut and we could get some coffee, or some wine and—" He trailed off, blushing furiously.

For the briefest of moments, Melissa thought about texting James and telling him that his surprise would have to wait as something had come up at work. But James had been known to come and see her anyway when she'd said she was busy; it would definitely be the end of the relationship if he found her drinking wine with Ian.

"That sounds great, it really does, but I've got plans tonight. Could you put it off until tomorrow maybe? Or Sunday? Or Monday? I'm free all those nights."

He gave her a small smile. "I'm sure I can save it up if you're interested."

"I am," she said. "Very."

When Ian reached the warden's hut, he found the answerphone flashing. He poured himself a cup of coffee before hitting the *Play* button. It was Stuart, the deer warden at nearby Lotherton Hall.

"Hey, Ian. It's just Stu. Look, I wanted to speak to you in person, so can you please give me a call when you get this? Thanks."

A shiver ran down Ian's spine. Telling himself not to jump the gun, he dialled Stuart's number. Stuart answered almost instantly.

"Hi, Stu. It's Ian. What's up?"

"Oh, hey. Thanks for calling back. Look, I wondered if you'd noticed anything weird about your herd recently."

"Weird how?"

"Just . . . weird," he replied, unhelpfully.

"I saw a rogue stag this morning," Ian said cautiously. "The tag had been ripped from its ear."

"Shit," Stuart muttered. Ian rode the subsequent silence. He could imagine Stuart sucking on his ginger moustache, the way he did when he was anxious. "Okay. Look, I'm going to send you something. I want you to watch it and delete it — promise?"

"I promise."

"I fucking mean it," Stuart growled.

"Then I fucking promise," Ian replied sharply.

"Right then. It's from a mate in Newcastle. He got called out to an . . . incident by a concerned member of the public, and he found the phone lying near . . . well, you'll see. He swiped it so the police couldn't take it away from him. Once you've watched the video, delete it and my email and clear out your trash and everything, alright?"

"Alright."

"Good. I'm sure it'll get to the press eventually, but for now, I want it kept quiet, okay?"

"Okay."

Without a word of goodbye, Stuart hung up. Ian took a few more sips of coffee, his stomach churning, before his inbox registered a new message. It was an email with no subject, no text, just a video attachment. With a slight tremble to his hands, Ian clicked on *Play*.

The opening scene was of a field with a stag pacing in the distance. The camera was shaking, and the wind made one hell of a noise, but Ian could just make out a man's voice.

"So, this is not a trick or a stunt, okay? That deer over there killed this man and was . . . eating him." The camera was pointed towards the floor where a bloody corpse lay partially scattered over the grass.

"I mean . . . shit. I mean, obviously deer eat meat, but never, in all my time as a warden have I ever . . . just look at him. He's been gored to death. You can see the . . ." The camera shook as the cameraman swapped hands and pointed to gouges in the corpse's shoulders. "You can see the holes where it impaled him with its antlers. I saw it lift him up and just toss him aside. And when the man hit the ground, it stamped on his head." The camera was angled so that the dead man's crushed skull was visible. "I've seen deer attack, of course, but nothing like this.

"I've called the police but there's something wrong with all this. There's a government lab nearby, and I heard how they've found the deer rooting around in the bin bags before now. It made me wonder," the man's voice dropped low, "what if there was something in there and the deer ate it and it messed him up? I mean, this guy's body had foam on it from the deer's mouth. It's gone now but maybe if I get a vial I — *shit*

shit!"

The camera tumbled to the floor, the lens pointing to the sky. The sound of a man's receding footsteps was heard then drowned out by the thundering of hooves. A huge shape blotted out the sky for a moment before the sound of hoofbeats faded into the distance. The video ended.

Ian stared at the computer screen, his shocked mind turning everything over. The cameraman had said it wasn't a prank, and the body had looked real enough, but could it really have been staged? Publicity for a new horror movie coming out maybe?

Yet at the forefront of his mind was the image of a stag, its ear tag gone, its antlers bloody.

He watched the video three more times, trying to zoom in on crucial bits. Then he fired up the internet and started his research.

Melissa had been hoping that Ian would drop by the café again, but he didn't. She'd even hoped to see the deer again, just so she could have an excuse to call him, but it made no reappearance.

When she finally turned the "open" sign to "closed", it was close to sunset. Betty had already left for bingo, so Melissa closed up then headed back to the car. The darkness pressed close; she kept looking around, expecting to see that deer again, but the only sign of life was a rat which ran across the path.

James had said to meet at 9pm, so she was able to go home, shower, and get changed. She was pulling up at the back entrance at 8:55pm. The night air was chill, so she waited in her car, listening to the radio, her windscreen steaming up. When it got to 9:15pm, she got out of the car and began walking around to keep warm. Through the trees, she could see the distant lights of the deer warden's hut. The thought of being in there with Ian and a bottle of wine was suddenly very appealing, but then she heard the crunch of tires on gravel and turned to find James parking his smart Audi next to her battered Fiesta.

"Sorry, sweetheart," he said, getting out. "I got held up at the office."

"I'm bloody freezing," she said, more crossly than she'd intended, "so whatever you've got planned had better be warm."

"Oh, I'll warm you right up," he said with a grin. A tingle ran though her; one of the main reasons she hadn't broken up with James was because of the sex. He'd never disappointed her, even when they'd been forced to do it in the cramped back seat of her Fiesta or when they'd had to be excessively quiet while her sister was visiting. Melissa would have been mortified if Kate had heard them, but James had been so slow and teasing without the bed squeaking even once.

James hauled a rucksack out of the trunk and tucked a blanket under his arm. Melissa raised an eyebrow. "A picnic?"

James grinned. "Sort of. But I didn't bring dessert. Maybe you and I could think of something sweet to end the meal with?"

The idea was appealing, not least because it was rife with danger. If she got caught, having sex outside on her employer's land— But the Johnsons were visiting friends, and while there was a security guard, he kept to the house and avoided the wood.

"Okay," she said. "But let's make it a short picnic, yeah? It really is bloody freezing."

Ian rubbed his eyes. His desk was littered with all the day's undone admin. He'd spent his time alternating between walking the woods and keeping an eye on the online news websites for any hint of the story breaking.

Perhaps the blood on the deer's antlers was from that original attack. Perhaps this wasn't even the same deer. The uncertainty was giving him a headache.

With a sigh, he retrieved a tin of beef ravioli from the cupboard. He'd have a quick bite to eat then do another circuit of the property. It troubled him that his own herd had not been in their usual places throughout the day. Something had upset them and had changed their routine. Of course, the presence of a new male could do that, especially one that smelt of blood. But it still didn't feel right.

When his food was ready, he sat down in front of the computer again. He had up on his browser a selection of videos he'd found across the web. One showed a deer gnawing on human bones that had been left outside a lab to measure the rate of human decomposition. He'd seen it before, of course, but now he watched it with a sense of dread. Other open tabs had videos of deer attacking passersby, but none of them indicated the same ferocity as the Newcastle video.

It was all very worrying and, as he spooned ravioli into his mouth, he vowed he'd walk the woods all night if that's what it took to get an answer.

The picnic had turned out to be little more than some shop-bought tapas and a bottle of wine, but James had been charming and had done things to her body that made her forget about the disappointing fare.

Now, one orgasm down, she sat astride him, grinding her hips against his, with him buried in her up to the hilt. They were both still fully clothed apart from her pants and tights because she hadn't been kidding when she'd said it was bloody cold. Thankfully, the sensations building inside her distracted her from the chilly air, but they were not enough to distract her from the stag watching them.

"Hey, what's the matter?" James asked as she froze mid-stroke. "Come on, sweetheart, don't—" then he, too, caught sight of the deer. He laughed. "Oh, is that it? Don't you like having an audience?" He raised himself on his arms, trying to catch her head and draw her in for a kiss. "All adds to the fun, doesn't it?"

She avoided his grasp; every muscle had gone rigid. The deer stepped towards them, completely unperturbed.

That's okay though, she thought anxiously. *I've seen loads of visitors get close to these animals and take picture of them. They must be really tame, that's all.*

She realised that it was foaming at the mouth when a glob of spittle elongated then fell to the ground. As it stepped closer, the camping lantern James had brought lit up its features. Its antlers were glistening and had intestine strung between them like grisly tinsel.

Don't run. Ian said not to run. Just back away slowly.

As gracefully as she could, Melissa climbed off James, ignoring his protestations. As he struggled to his feet and tucked himself away, the stag turned its head to watch him.

It's sizing us up, deciding who to go for.

"All this fuss," James was grumbling, "it's only—"

"Look at the antlers you idiot," Melissa hissed. "They're covered in blood."

James stared, his eyes widening. "It'll just be from another deer, yeah?" he said uncertainly. "That's what antlers are for, aren't they? Attacking and stuff."

"Well, I work here, and I've never seen a deer with that much blood on its antlers before. It's not normal. Come on, let's just go."

"Fine. Let me just pack up and—"

"Leave it," she insisted, bending down to grab her shoes.

"No way! That blanket came from John Lewis. I'm not leaving it here for some animal to shit on."

Ignoring James, Melissa slipped on her shoes and started to back away, never taking her eyes off the stag. The fact that it's gaze was locked on James did nothing to ease her rising trepidation.

James straightened, the picnic mostly packed away. "See? It hasn't done anything. It's just a big dumb beast that was probably attracted to the food. It'll soon wander off. Watch. Go on!" He moved towards the animal, waving his arms. "Shoo! Go away!"

The stag lowered its head and charged, covering the twenty feet between them frighteningly fast. James tried to dive out of the way, but the deer angled its head, following his movements to impale him on the end of its

103

antlers. Melissa screamed; James was only able to give out a bloody, bubbling groan as the air whistled out of his punctured lungs. The deer raised its head, lifting James off the floor. James's eyes widened in agony and he gripped the antlers, trying to haul himself off them.

The stag shook its head, tossing him to and fro like a rag doll until James went flying. With a grunt of expelled air, he hit a tree trunk then slithered to the ground.

As the stag shook its head once more, blood rained from its antlers onto the ground. It walked over to where James lay wheezing. The animal looked down, as if considering some weighty matter. Then it reared up and brought its front hooves down on James's chest. There was the crack of ribs and the thunk of hooves hitting wet meat; James's whole body spasmed with the force of the blow before going limp and lifeless, his head slumped to the side.

With incongruous grace, the stag stepped to the side, lifting its feet out of James's body, a trail of gore coming with them. After giving one hoof a cursory lick, the deer buried its muzzle in James's ruined ribcage and began to tear apart his steaming organs.

Melissa's hand had shot to her mouth, holding back whimpers as she watched her boyfriend being devoured.

Got to go. Must leave. Can't help him. The blood—

Don't think of that. Just go. I can't believe . . .

Concentrate! Back up. Don't run.

As she backed away, Melissa accidentally kicked over the camping lamp. It clattered to the ground, sending shadows swirling around the trees.

The deer paused in its meal. After a long moment, it turned to look at her, blood and froth dribbling from its mouth.

Melissa turned and ran.

Ian stared down at the dead rambler. The man's head had been smashed to a pulp, his brains mushed into the soggy ground. His clothing had been torn and the flesh underneath had been partially eaten.

Digging out his phone, Ian tried to take a picture but his hands were shaking so badly that he couldn't get a decent shot. He closed his eyes and breathed deeply. Thankfully, the remains were several hours old and the cold breeze kept the stench of decay subdued.

Try not to think of it as a man, he told his whirling brain. *Of course, it is a man, but try to see it as you would another deer. Sort yourself out enough to get a decent shot.* He guessed that if he called the police, this would be hushed up just like Newcastle. There was no way something like that could happen without it hitting the national newspapers, so the story must have been suppressed.

Feeling a little calmer, he opened his eyes and stared at the bright, starry sky for a few moments to soothe him a little further. When he looked down again, he could almost view the body with detachment — at least enough to take a decent photo. He took close-ups of the brain matter and the man's canteen, which was dented and sported a perfect hoof print right in the centre.

As he was checking through the photos, wondering whether to send them to Stuart or the police first, a scream shattered the night. It was followed by a distant thud, as of something large hitting a tree.

His heart hammering, he shoved his phone into his pocket and raced off towards the sound, clutching his shotgun tightly.

Right up until the water reached Melissa's waist, she had been convinced that it was a good idea to run into the large woodland pond. As she'd fled, she'd looked at every passing tree, trying to calculate if she could scramble up far enough to escape those bloody antlers. But she'd never climbed a tree in her life, and making this her first attempt didn't seem wise.

She remembered that Ian had told her that you could use a tree as a barrier between you and an aggressive deer, but when glancing back at the huge beast closing in behind her, it seemed impossible that any tree could provide an adequate barrier.

Then she'd seen the pond — the deep, moonlit pond, and inspiration struck. Deer couldn't swim. She'd be safe there. So she'd headed in that direction. The relief she'd felt when she first splashed into the pond had been almost orgasmic. But then she'd nearly slipped twice on the slimy stones underfoot, and very quickly she'd begun to shiver.

Now, with the water almost up to her chest, she carefully turned round and looked behind her. The stag was there, standing on the edge of the pond, staring at her. Emerging from the trees behind him were more deer, some with white froth glistening around their mouths too.

The stag tilted its head, watching her with one bloodshot eye, and Melissa abruptly wondered where she'd got the idea that deer couldn't swim. Suddenly, the pond seemed a very stupid idea indeed.

Tentatively, the stag stepped into the water. The slimy stones were no kinder to the deer, and it scrabbled for purchase. Melissa felt a flicker of hope as the creature backed out of the water; it tried another entry point with the same result. Its glare told Melissa that it was only a matter of time before it found a way in. Could she grab those bloody antlers and force its head under the water, drowning it before it gored her?

"Melissa? Is that you?" Ian was advancing slowly towards the pond from the left, a shotgun levelled at the stag.

"Ian! Thank god. This deer's not right. It's the one I saw. It hurt James — no, it killed him. I think it killed him. And I ran. And this seemed like a good idea but—" Her chattering teeth made any further words illegible, but Ian nodded grimly.

"It's alright. Just swim slowly towards me and climb out, okay?" He had made it to the edge of the pond; his eyes never left the stag, which returned his stare with a cool malevolence.

Melissa began to swim towards Ian, splitting her attention between him and the stag which was stamping its front hoof on the ground. Climbing out was even harder than wading in now her legs and feet had gone numb with cold. As soon as she was in range, she grabbed hold of Ian's arm. The weight of her sent the shotgun swaying upwards. The stag lowered its head, steam billowing from its nostril, but Ian swiftly had the gun trained on it again and the creature snorted in irritation, flecks of foam and droplets of blood splattering into the pond.

"Easy now," Ian said. Melissa couldn't decide if he was talking to her or the animal, and her teeth were still chattering too much to ask. The night air was only deepening the cold of her wet skin. "We're heading back to the warden's hut, okay?" he asked her.

She managed a strained, "Y-yes," and they started backing away from the pond.

Ian's gaze was fixed on the stag, but Melissa's eyes were flicking across the deer that were circling them in the trees.

God, there's bloody hundreds of them. She'd always considered them majestic and beautiful, but now they seemed sleek and sinister, their black eyes filled with hatred.

"Ian, t-there's m-more. Look," she stuttered.

Ian's head moved only a fraction. "Are there any right behind us?" he asked. The stag had been matching them step for step.

"N-No."

"Well, that's good. Let me know if they are, alright? Because if they—"

With an animal screech, one of the does charged forward, froth spraying from its mouth. Ian swung the gun in one smooth movement and shot the creature in the chest. The doe's legs buckled, its momentum carrying it forward so that it crashed into them, knocking them both down. Melissa screamed as she fell. As the world upended itself, she saw the stag lower its head and charge.

Ian had been half-expecting an attack from one of the surrounding deer. Any other day, it would have sounded impossible; that was the kind of pack behaviour you got from predators. But the minute Ian had entered that clearing, had seen the stag, Melissa, and the deer circling them, he'd known that he was dealing with the impossible.

Although he swung the gun round with admirable speed, the doe had been so close that its death throes had toppled him and Melissa. Even worse, they ended up on the floor with Melissa pinning his gun to the floor, just as the stag started to charge.

He bloody knows! was the thought that blazed across Ian's mind. *He knows I can't fire. He planned it.*

But there was no time for crazy assumptions. Ian had to act or they'd both be dead.

There was no way to get the gun free in time, so he did the next best thing. As Melissa scrambled to her feet, Ian bunched his legs up and shoved hard, sending her flying and using the momentum to roll himself the other way. A split second later, the stag's hooves hammered over the ground where they'd just been lying.

The creature bellowed in frustration, fighting its momentum and trying to turn. Ian crawled over to where his gun was lying, bringing it up and round as quickly as he could. But panic got the better of him and he fired too soon, clipping the stag's flank. The animal skidded and Ian dived out of the way, cursing and righting himself as quickly as he could before fumbling in his pocket for two more cartridges.

Bleeding from its side and panting heavily, the stag turned to face him once more. Its eyes were crazed. As the beast started forward once more, the cartridge slipped from Ian's fingers to the ground. Looking up at the oncoming monster, Ian knew he was out of luck and time.

God, I hope it's quick. What a shitty way to go.

A branch flashed out of the darkness, slamming into the stag's face. The deer screamed and shied away. Melissa, who'd been wielding the branch, wasn't quick enough to get out of the way of its thundering hooves; and her foot was trampled. She fell to the ground, shrieking, as the deer furiously shook his head from side to side, trying to dislodge the branch tangled in its antlers.

Swiftly, Ian knelt down, retrieved the cartridge, and slotted it into the second barrel before snapping the gun shut. Finally free of the branch, the stag turned back to Ian. A deep gouge ran across one eye, the eyeball open and spilling jelly. The stag didn't appear to care; it simply meant that its remaining eye was filled with twice the hatred.

As the animal lowered its head, Ian raised the gun. It had already broken into a run when he fired; at such close range, the entire section of skull between its antlers exploded. The beast's head jerked back with the violence of the shot, and then the stag was falling to the ground, its life and madness instantly extinguished.

Ian walked over and shot it once more in the head, just to be sure.

Melissa's foot was agony. Every time she tried to put weight on it, a bolt of white pain arced through her leg. Emotions pummelled her as she and Ian staggered through the night together: anger at herself for being stupid enough to get trodden on; intense gratitude that Ian was pretty much carrying her right now; relief that the monster was dead; and fear of the half-seen shapes keeping pace with them among the trees.

"Almost there," Ian muttered. By Melissa's count, he'd been saying that for an hour at least, but the pain made everything seem harder and longer, so she couldn't honestly say just how long they had really been stumbling through the wood.

Eventually, the lights of the hut appeared through the trees and they really were almost there. Just as they were approaching the door, a dark shape of a doe dashed in front of them. Every muscle in her body tensed, fearing another attack, but the deer was gone in a flash, and then Ian had the door open and was pushing her through. No sooner had he shut it than something slammed into it from the other side.

"Will that door hold? It looks pretty flimsy," she asked. There was another impact, and she saw the wood shudder.

"I hope so," he said in such a grim manner that she gained no comfort from it. "Let me take a look at that foot."

Melissa nearly fainted at the pain as he touched her foot, and it proved too much when he tried to take off her shoes. When the lights had finally stopped flashing in her vision, she found Ian sitting there, biting his bottom lip.

"It looks bad, but I'm in a bit of a bind, you see. You need an ambulance, but I have to call other people first. Can you imagine what would happen to the paramedics if they tried to fight their way through those deer?" As if to emphasise his point, there was another collision outside.

"Look, I've got some really strong painkillers here somewhere. Take those and we'll elevate your leg, and then I'll make some calls. As soon as it's safe to do so, I *promise* I will call an ambulance."

Ian was already walking away as he spoke; he returned a few minutes later with a packet of tablets with a long, unpronounceable name on the front. Ian handed her a leaflet detailing all the side effects.

"I don't give a shit," Melissa said. "Just give me the highest dose, preferably with some vodka, okay?"

Ian poured her a glass of water then gave her one tablet. When she glared at him, he popped another out of the strip before sliding it back into the packet.

Melissa forced them down; the pain was making her nauseous and her stomach rebelled at even two mouthfuls of water. But she didn't throw up, and gradually the pain lessened and the world became blissfully hazy around the edges.

It was 3am before Ian's calls finally bore fruit. The police turned up, as did an ambulance, and some guys from the CDC. Most worryingly, two men and a woman, all in jeans and t-shirts, turned up as well. They couldn't be older than their mid-twenties; one of the men (boys, Ian thought) had greasy hair, the other had thick glasses, and the woman had her hair pulled back in a ferociously tight ponytail that made her frown even more pronounced. Their expressions ranged from distaste to fascination at what was going on.

The trio hovered near the CDC guys but were clearly not part of that team. Yet Brian, who worked for the CDC, went and spoke to them in low voices after he'd talked to Ian.

Shit. Are those the kind of people running the show now? No wonder the world is going to hell and deer are eating people.

As he'd expected, his computer and phone were bagged and confiscated. He felt immensely relieved that he'd transferred his pictures to a memory stick and hidden that under a loose floorboard. As the man from the CDC took away his phone, Melissa raised an eyebrow and said, in a voice slurred by drugs, "Aw, how am I supposed to call you for a date now?"

Despite the situation, he found himself laughing. "A date? Seriously? After what happened tonight?"

She held out her hand and he took it — mostly to stop her from sliding off the seat. "Course. You're my night white. I mean, my white knight." She giggled and squeezed his hand.

Suddenly, ponytail-girl was next to him, peering at his hand. "Is that cut fresh?" she asked, pointing at a graze near his thumb.

"Yeah, caught it on branches or someth—hey!" He'd been trying to slide the sleeve of his jacket down but she'd grabbed his wrist and brought her face close to the wound.

"Mike! I'm gonna need a swab!" she called over her shoulder. She smiled at Ian; from the painful way her facial muscles twitched, it was clear she didn't smile often. "Nothing to worry about, sir, I'm sure. So long as you weren't bitten or got any deer blood in the wound."

"I think I'd remember that," he said. But even as he spoke, he was thinking of that spray of blood and brains. His coat was still sticky from it; his face had been drenched; why would his hand have remained clean? But it had to be. The thought of being infected by whatever had driven those deer crazy was just too horrible to contemplate.

Greasy-guy handed her a swab. As she prepared to take a sample, she smiled again. "I'm sure it'll be fine," she said. Her tone was unconvincing, and Ian felt sure that the horrors of the night weren't over yet.

TUPPENCE A BAG

Steve Toase

THE TOXIC AVIAN archaeology below Zoe's feet was not her concern. A stratigraphy of dead birds bone bare and time plucked were of no interest to her, despite the depth of time marked in dishevelled feathers and piles of shit.

Her job was to catalogue the factory's architectural features, the old ironwork and the windowed office set up to allow the managers all those years ago to constantly observe their workers. To photograph the game boards scratched into floors and triangles of cigarette butts in hidden corners.

Sweat ran down the neck of her chem. suit. She positioned the tripod and adjusted the camera, letting the light meter settle. Changing her footing, hollow bones popped beneath her boot and she winced.

Footsteps echoed from above where Maggie was recording the upper floor of the building. They'd been working together for a couple of years, mostly alongside each other, but the factory was vast and the Historic Building Survey had a strict deadline, one not made easier by the state of the place.

Time had made the building treacherous. Metal had been stolen by the desperate, industrial waste fly-tipped by the careless. Over everything lay a carpet of dead birds, dander, a fine powder from their rotting wings, dangerous enough to need protective equipment normally worn while tearing out asbestos.

Making a record in her notebook, Zoe picked up the camera and tripod, moving them a couple of metres to photograph an original door which had survived the factory's long afterlife pretty much intact.

Above her the dead birds' descendents called to each other, unaffected by the human intruders in their kingdom. How many bird generations had been born and died since the building was abandoned. Five? Fifty? She noted down the photographs and moved the camera once more to record some 1950's worker graffiti.

The cooing reminded her of cold Saturday mornings waiting at her grandad's pigeon loft for his birds to come into view, crest the roofs of the estate and come to rest.

When the old man died no one bothered to check on the birds. None of her relatives cared. She was away at university at the time. By the time of the funeral, all his champions had starved. She buried the small frail corpses in the woods where her grandad always took his dead birds.

Some of the family wanted to burn them or leave them out for the foxes. No way her grandad would have put up with that. The feathers brushed against her hands as she placed them in shallow holes and covered them back up with soil, bands still in place on their ankles. None of the factory pigeons birds had numbers, feral and free to live on crumbling window sills and die in vast burial mounds of their own creation.

"Zoe, can you come up for a moment?" Maggie's voice was loud and muffled. Several birds took to the wing at the disturbance, feathers strobing sunlight as they changed perch. Zoe reached into her site bag for a small handful of seeds, casting them against the wall. They hit, scattering, ready for the pigeons above to find later. They might be ragged but they still deserved to eat.

Turning off the camera, Zoe crossed the bone littered floor. Flakes of dried pigeon skin in the air swirled away from her. Checking the strength of each stair before committing, she made her way to the floor above.

Maggie stood leaning against the wall, mask hanging from her neck and a cigarette hanging from her lips. She pointed to the far end of the room and nodded.

"I've no idea how they got up here, but I need to move them so I can get some clear shots of the wall."

Several barrels had been stacked under the eaves, any safety labels long faded and rotted as the metal itself became corroded by time.

Zoe walked across for a closer look. Over the years the seams around several of the lids had separated, becoming crusted with white yellow foam.

"They look pretty far gone," Zoe said.

"Still need to move them," Maggie said, crushing her cigarette out against the stone wall and dropping the filter into a small metal tin. There was no question that they would do it. The chain of command might be small, but it was still there. Maggie was the Historic Building Surveyor for the Archaeology Unit and Zoe was her assistant.

Nominally it was a training position. The main lessons over the past few months had been that old buildings are as dangerous for what's in them as what state they're in, and Maggie had a very loose relationship with health and safety. But it meant Zoe had a job when the usual archaeology site work came to an end, and she was mostly inside during the winter months, even if she was encased in a paper suit that meant she sweated twice as much as usual.

Maggie repositioned her mask and slid her hands into a pair of old gardening gloves then nodded to the waiting barrels.

Standing either side they walked the first container across the room, then the second. The third was a little heavier, but finally moved and they stacked it next to the first two.

"Only five more to go," Maggie said. Zoe gave her a thumbs up and was glad the mask hid her expression.

The fourth barrel did not move with gentle persuasion.

"Bit more force. After three," Maggie said. Zoe nodded and felt along the edge of the metal to get a better grip. "One. Two. Three."

Afterwards Zoe wasn't sure who fucked up. With a wrench they pulled the barrel to one side. The weight inside shifted, sending it clattering to the wooden floor, impact tearing away the lid. Black tar-like liquid seeped out, pooling on the floor. Where the barrel had corroded to its neighbours its movement tore a hole in the others, now also leaking a black viscous substance.

"Over here," Maggie said, standing by the stairs. The leak covered most of the floor and was starting to drop through the floorboards. Zoe stepped around until she was beside her boss then followed her down.

Back on the factory floor, Maggie gestured toward the main entrance. Zoe followed, glancing behind. The substance was now dripping from the ceiling to rain black on the dead birds below, leaving a thin black sheen over feather and bone alike and pooling in empty eye sockets. The early afternoon sunlight reflected back and Zoe couldn't shake the feeling that the dead pigeons were looking at her.

Outside, they walked to the Land Rover, pulled back their hoods and took off their masks. Unlocking the door, Maggie reached in and turned on the radio, grabbed a pack of cigarettes, took one out, lit it and closed her eyes.

"I'm sorry Maggie," Zoe said.

"Not your fault," Maggie said, tapping ash on the floor. "You weren't to know that they were so corroded. That's on me."

"Still," Zoe said. "Sorry."

"Honestly, not your fault," Maggie said, taking a last drag. "Where did you leave the camera?"

"Downstairs on the left," Zoe said.

"I need to grab my kit. It's beside the bottom of the stairs and I'll get yours on the way out."

"I'll come in too."

"No need for both of us. You do some paperwork or something. I won't be long."

Zoe finished stripping off the paper suit and sat down in the passenger seat. Truth was there was no paperwork to do. Reaching for her site bag, she slid her hand past her tools for a small bag of snacks.

The radio was loud enough for her not to notice the noise at first. Even though the building was old, and the original owner powerful enough to not care about noise pollution, the walls were still good at muffling any activity within.

Zoe recognised the sound, the same as when a fox got near her grandad's pigeon loft; the sound of wing against wing and panicked birds flying into each other.

Climbing out, she finished eating, grabbed a fresh chem. suit and mask, and dragged them on over her clothes. Now the sound was worse, punctuated by percussive echoes against the stone walls.

Out in the sun the protective suit was far too hot and Zoe walked over to be in the shade of the factory. Close up, the sound was deafening. She pulled the mask into place and opened the door. Above her several birds flew out. She ignored their bid for freedom. It took a few seconds for her eyes to adjust to the darkness within the building.

The whole floor rippled, feathers and bone straining against layers of droppings. Even through the mask she smelt the acrid burn of disturbed decades old piles of shit.

The whole mass of dead birds was covered in black sludge. Several cavities had been torn through the mound of the dead. She glanced up. The air was thick with dove dust, swirling in the shadows, and above the dust the pigeons themselves.

Some were feral birds, descendants of the dead. Those looked ragged enough, torn and beaten by the ravages of city scavenging. There were other pigeons on the wing above her far worse.

Even from a distance she saw feathers missing from their tails, heads bare bone, empty eye sockets staring from above broken beaks. Some had no plumage at all, strands of muscle dangling from yellowed skeletons. Zoe became so transfixed by how they were staying aloft that she did not notice the screaming until it was too loud to ignore.

Zoe barely made out the figure of Maggie lying at the bottom of the stairs. Starting to run, she ignored the sound of her work boots cracking hollow bones.

Up close she saw the reason Maggie was so hard to recognise. Her boss was covered in dead pigeons. From head to toe they clung to her, claws slicing through her paper suit, now blossoming with blood. Several pigeons had tangled skinless legs in her hair and were scraping their beaks through her forehead to the bone beneath. Another had buried its head in her eye socket, scraping around inside. Maggie's arm lay stretched out to one side. A single bird nested in her hand as if waiting for its brood to emerge. The lack of feathers and muscle meant any chance of raising fledglings was a distant memory. The dead pigeons looked up at Zoe's approach.

She had no plan. Shoo them away? Give first aid? Drag Maggie toward the exit and hope the flock took flight?

They stared at her getting closer. A black tar-like substance seeped out of hollow bones.

The pigeons did not move. These were no longer fretful creatures begging crumbs below city benches. Already dead, the pigeons had nothing left to fear. Certainly not from her.

The door was a straight run behind her. Even walking she could reach it before the birds could reach her. There was nothing left to do for Maggie except recover her corpse at another time. That wouldn't happen unless she got out of the factory and raised the alarm. Grinding her foot into the decades thick layer of bones, feathers and bird shit, she readied herself to run.

The ground shifted below her. Zoe barely managed to keep upright. Between where she stood and the door, the whole floor was moving, rippling. Piece by bird shaped piece, the floor rose into the air.

Some of the corpses were skeletal, held together by the stretch of dried tendons, some caked with a gritty residue and the feathers of other dead pigeons. Close by her feet, two pigeons welded together by death crawled up from under a pile of rotten wood. By the wall several mummified squabs clung to the stone.

The air was thick with the dead. Every few seconds more and more dragged themselves free of the burial mound, cutting off her escape.

The manager's office was raised off the ground and sealed. None of the pigeons had managed to colonise it. Not looking back, she ran to her side, stamped across resurrected corpses, feeling them shatter with every footstep, the flock of those who could fly growing with every moment.

She felt them in the air behind her, wings spraying her with flaked skin. Reaching the steps up to the manager's office, something gripped the back of her chem. suit and she flinched, reaching back to brush it off. Another pecked through her glove, trying to clamp the tendons in the back of her fingers. Screaming, she flung it away to one side, watching the already dead pigeon land on the factory floor, climb to its feet and take flight once more.

The office door opened inwards. Zoe ran inside and slammed it shut behind her. Two pigeons clung to her suit, tearing holes with their beaks, trying to get at the warm meat below. As fast as she dared, she grabbed them, opened the door a little and threw both back into the factory.

The pigeons kept coming.

Zoe walked around the hexagonal room, staring out in one direction after another. The flock was concentrated on one side, wave after wave battering themselves against the windows, succeeding in doing nothing apart from smearing the glass. Between the feathers she saw Maggie's body on the floor. Several pigeons had returned to the paper suited corpse and were tearing through damp muscle to the white glistening bone beneath.

Designed for insidious surveillance of workers by management, the 360 degree visibility gave Zoe a chance to weigh up her options. If only the resurrected dead would stop flying at the windows, then there might be a chance to concentrate and plan a way out. There was no way for them to shatter through the reinforcement; the factory bosses all those years ago were too concerned about tools "accidentally" slipping out of hands to use normal glass.

From above a new sound joined the cacophony of feathers and bones, a sound that took her straight back to her grandad's pigeon loft.

A pigeon in distress was the worst sound in the world. Most died quickly, either by bullet, jaws or a quick twist of the neck when they were beyond saving, but a bird dying slowly? They made sure the whole world knew.

She saw them, the already dead mobbing the still living. Dragging the victims to the factory floor, they pinned them in place to the concrete, and plucked out the tiny hearts. Slowly but surely they dripped the black chemicals into the chest cavity, feathers bowing out with the pressure.

One by one they slaughtered them all, until no living birds remained in the factory. Some tried to flee for the gaps they used to venture into town and scavenge, but the corpse pigeons knew and were there first, bringing the frightened creatures down with sheer weight, five six hanging off each wing. Soon there were no living or dead, just the recent dead and the ancient dead.

Around the office the corpses never stopped flying, until the newly murdered pigeons were ready to take flight, then the flock settled to the factory floor. One by one the plump feathered birds rose away from their killers. They weren't elegant, as if they only half remembered how to fly. Sunlight came through shattered tiles and glistened off the black chemicals coating their eyes.

They came to rest on the office roof. She saw their tail feathers hanging over the edge, fringing the office. One by one they emptied their bowels.

Droppings streaked down the glass, smearing and coagulating until Zoe could no longer see outside, glass beginning to steam and melt. On every side the recently dead defecated down the windows, their chemically enhanced shit weakening the barrier.

Unsure what to do, Zoe stood in the middle of the room and watched the glass thin. The flock took to the wing once more and rotting bird after rotting bird careered into the windows, pulling away melted glass fused to bare bone.

Inside the office Zoe looked for somewhere to shelter. The room had long been stripped of any furnishings. The roosting pigeons above still emptied themselves while their ancestors flung themselves again and again at the weakened windows.

It took a moment for Zoe to notice that all their efforts were concentrated on the five main windows, the narrow frosted glass in the door making her almost invisible to the birds beyond.

Quiet and slow, she unlatched the door and glanced outside, trying to estimate the distance to the main entrance. Now all the pigeons were trying to break the glass, maybe they were distracted enough with the task to let her escape. Maybe they were too focussed on the office to notice her.

More and more corrosive bird droppings dripped down the windows, bones separated from wings and ribcages staying in place. The flock might catch her before she got out. She might fall down the stairs and be feasted upon like Maggie. One thing was for sure though. If she stayed where she was it was only a matter of time before they got through. She needed to prepare.

First she stripped her chem. suit down to her waist, took off her jumper and put the protective clothing back on. Never taking her eye off the dead birds she wrapped the jumper around her head, then placed her hand on the door handle and waited. There was a rhythm to their attacks, their waves, like they were thinking with one intent. Hive mind. She waited. On the far side the glass began to crack. She waited. The first bird got its beak inside. She waited. The hole was big enough for the creature to get in, losing the last of its feathers on the way. Zoe opened the door and ran.

The flock was so focussed on getting into the office they did not notice she was no longer there until she was almost at the exit. She risked a look over her shoulder. Most were trapped, flapping around the office trying to kill someone no longer there. When they realised their victim had fled the sheer crush of them all trying to leave at once sent many to the floor, too broken to be able to take to the wing. Enough escaped though, soon joined by the still feathered recently living.

Reaching the entrance, she wrenched open the door, not caring about splinters tearing up her hands, and ran to the Land Rover, shutting herself inside. She rested her head against the dash and waited for her breathing to settle before taking off her mask.

Outside was a bright summer's day. The park across from the factory was packed with people finishing work early and making the best of the weather. Some were feeding ducks in the small lake and Zoe saw grey feathers in the trees, She turned back to look at the factory. The roof was the same grey.

Hundreds of pigeons crowded the gutter. Some had been dead for decades, in the daylight she saw how truly ragged they were, others killed and resurrected only moments before. Black streaks blistered the stonework.

More and more gathered, squeezing out of gaps under the eaves, through broken tiles and through the entrance that, in her rush to escape, she had not shut properly behind her.

One by one they took to the wing, darkening the sky as they flew across to the park, streaks of shit corroding metal railings and tarmac alike. Several emptied their bowels onto the 4x4's roof and she listened to the paint bubbling.

The pigeons did not attack the people. First they took to the trees, taking down the other pigeons they found. In the middle of family picnics and keep fit sessions they pinned the living birds to the grass and transformed them into living corpses like themselves. The screaming started off as disgust but soon turned to terror.

The pigeons mobbed the people one by one. Some were torn apart by precise beaks, others blinded as birds emptied their bowels of the toxic sludge. At least one was choked to death as bird after bird forced their way into his open mouth stretching their victim's throat as they reached his stomach and pecked their way out from the inside.

Zoe watched some people try to escape to be pushed to the ground by the weight of wings. In the street between the factory and the park drivers abandoned their cars, unsure of where to run. The flock picked them off one by one.

Above the streets, the air darkened with oil coloured feathers as fragments of the flock took to the air once more. Zoe watched them assemble into a swirling mass, then split once more as they spotted new targets. Several smears of bird droppings hit the windscreen and, almost lazily, the glass turned liquid and thinned. Staying still would not save her. The only chance to survive was to leave.

Trying to still the shake in her hand, Zoe started the ignition. On the other side of the fence, a family lay choking on the pavement, mouths clogged with thick grey dust.

She dare not get out to open the site fencing. Instead, she drove at the gap, pushing the panels apart with the vehicle, hollow rubber boot holding the panels dragged until the wire buckled and fell leaving a gap big enough to drive through. Everywhere pigeons feasted on the crowds.

Bodies lay across the road and pavement, outlines distorted by fluttering wings, some feathered and some bare bones. Zoe knew there was no saving the fallen. She closed her eyes, took a breath and drove over the obstructions, turning up the radio to drown out the sounds of bodies, both small and large, splitting under the weight of the vehicle.

Beyond the park, beyond the factory, beyond the streets that surrounded them, everything felt normal. There was no panic, no sense of what was coming, the only sign was emergency vehicles streaming in the opposite direction. Zoe glanced in the rear view mirror. Beyond the blue lights, the sky was black with birds looking for their next victims, and the next birds to increase the flock.

The breeze was starting to pick up the cloud of dried skin now, swirling it past the factory and park. She watched it drift across people and cars alike, falling like Saharan sand. The coughing was delayed. Soon pedestrians began falling to their knees gasping for breath.

Traffic mounted the kerb to let police and ambulances through. Zoe took her chance and drove through the gaps. On the radio, the music finished leaving vague news reports of some kind of attack. Eye witnesses did not describe an explosion, just a thrumming sound and a grey powder. How do you describe the sound of thousands of dead pigeons taking to the sky? People stumbled out of the immediate area covered in scratches and burns, unable to describe what happened. Zoe carried on driving. Soon everyone would have the same idea.

The screams were getting louder, closer. She risked another glance behind. The grey mass in the sky was larger, glimpses of red on beaks and the white of bone. There was one place she could go to get away from the stench of blood and muscle and bird shit that was following her through the streets.

Time had taken its toll on the pigeon loft, wooden panels rotted and long since split. Chicken wire hung down in lazy curls as if the whole structure was some kind of overripe fruit. Above her the sky was clear, In the distance the flock was expanding over the town as they found more birds to resurrect. She wondered how long it would be until they found the corpses so carefully buried in the woods, pecked away the soil and gifted them the half-life of the undead. She wondered how long until her grandad's champions returned to the skies, until they remembered the homes they left so long ago. She would wait there until they returned. She owed her grandad that much. Across the city the sky was a mass of feathers, the buildings below covered in fine dust, the streets in corpses. Not long until they found their way back home. Not long at all.

BULLIES

Amanda DeBord

TEN-YEAR-OLD POTTER KNEW what he'd seen
in the creek. He was at that age where there was
still magic in the world, but he could feel it
slipping away. He could see it in his friends'
waning interests in ghosts and spaceships, and he
began to know that the adults had never even
believed those stories in the first place. But that
day walking in the creek, he knew he'd seen a
bullfrog as big as a beagle.

Thirty years later, he could still see its
sun-pale corpse, bobbing belly-up in the muck
along the bank. That part of the creek was full of
frogs; every step brought a tiny *croak!* and a
splash as his presence disturbed a spring peeper
from its hiding spot. Every ten or so steps, and
the ripple of his footfalls shook out a low *jugrum*
from a bullfrog sinking down in the water. If you
heard two dozen bullfrogs on a creek-walking day,
you might see two. But Potter saw this one. He
was past it before his mind processed the image,
and he picked up his feet in a stutter-step, as if
he'd seen a snake, spooked by the thought of
touching water that had touched—*that*. Stretched
out on its back, mouth open. It had to have been
at least two feet long and nearly a foot across, the
jaw so wide that it nearly formed a square angle
at the tip. Its legs twitched and wiggled from the
ripples in the water, as if it were still alive, but the
minnows nibbling at its eyes told the truth. Potter
kept walking. He didn't turn back to look. He
didn't really *want* to see it again, but he especially

didn't want to look back and see that it was gone.

At least the mosquitos weren't biting. Potter sat on his tailgate and took another unsatisfying drag off his cigarette. Mark was nearly an hour late. On any other day he might have appreciated the down time. It was rare anymore that he got to just sit by a pond and smoke, alone with his thoughts. But Lord it was hot. The afternoon heat shimmered off the surface of the pond. Without looking at the weather, Potter knew it was another record-breaker. Temperatures above 100 and how many days now without rain? Either way, he was seeing Marianne tonight and would like to at least shower off the sweat and grit before he went. Fifteen minutes more and he'd leave, call the boss man on the way back into town and tell him some bullshit excuse. He was pissed at Mark, but he'd never throw him under the bus. They could just as easily do the count tomorrow.

Jugrum.

Potter spit on the ground. "Yeah, you better celebrate, fucker. We're coming for you and your friends tomorrow." The frog didn't respond.

Mark had all the gigs and nets and buckets in his truck. That was their arrangement – Mark carried the dirty stuff in his dirty truck, Potter carried the paperwork (and an iPad now) and filled out the reports. They were supposed to be counting bullfrogs. Specifically, egg-heavy lady bullfrogs. There had been an absolute *explosion* of bullfrogs this summer, and the state Department of Conservation bigwigs were tired of fielding questions. So they put Potter and Mark, the Brothers Slime, the best wetland biologists in Emmet County (the only wetland biologists in Emmet County), on the case.

It was odd, Potter mused as he climbed back

in his truck. Rural Wisconsin fish and wildlife work was pretty uneventful. Annual counts of all the creepy-crawlies that most people didn't give a second thought to, surveys of a few endangered species that most people hadn't heard of, and maybe the occasional fish with a misshapen fin made up the entirety of Potter's summers. But this year was all frogs. It was all anyone talked about. *"Have you heard all those frogs?"* What unnerved Potter was what you *didn't* hear. Bugs. Annoying as they may be, you grow accustomed to the evening bug sounds. This summer there were hardly any bugs. It was stiflingly silent in the twilight, until the chorus started up. Spring peepers and tree frogs, croaking toads and the throaty baritone of the bullfrogs. So many bullfrogs. If you were outside at night, the thrumming, echoing *jugrum* pulsed in your ears until it made you dizzy.

At least the corn farmers were happy. More frogs meant fewer grasshoppers meant hardly any chewed up leaves on this year's crop. The livestock farmers, on the other hand . . . something was going on with the county's pigs and goats. The cows were being left alone – it seemed to only affect the animals that were closer to the ground. Thankfully that wasn't Potter's area. He said a little prayer for the Farm Bureau workers every time he saw another field of dead pigs.

Potter dialed Mark as he pulled away from the pond and got his voice mail again. "Hey dick hole! Thanks for standing me up today. Imma drive by your house and if you're out on the boat drinking, we're going to have words. I—" *beepbeep.* Potter had another call. He switched over.

"Hello?"

"Potter? Where you at?"

"Hey Boss. Just leaving the office." Potter hoped to God Boss-man wasn't calling from the office himself. "Just finishing up the algae reports."

"I thought you all were checking the frogs out at Norman's pond today."

"No, sir. That's tomorrow. I figured the state'd be looking for these water-quality numbers more than a bunch of dead frogs in a bucket."

"You ain't wrong. But listen. You hear from Mark today? He's not answering my calls, not even on his house phone."

Mark, you asshole, Potter thought. *You're really going to make me lie for you, aren't you?* "Yeah, me and him were just —"

"Alright, alright. Well wherever he is, tell him to call me in the next 20 minutes or he's going to be filling out algae reports until Christmas."

"Yessir. Have a good evening, sir."

Potter hung up the phone and called Mark again. Voice mail. He was going to have to drive by the house. Boss-man's bark was worse than his bite, but Potter at least wanted to warn Mark that he was in the crosshairs.

Potter felt an unpleasant drop in his stomach as he turned up Mark's gravel drive. The front door was open. Tully, Mark's little rat terrier, romped in the front yard and yapped at Potter's tires as he approached the house.

"Mark?" Potter called, walking toward the door. "Where's your boy, Tully? Too many tall boys for breakfast and forgot to latch the door again?" Tully just looked at him, tongue lolling out of his happy mouth.

"Mark? You in here bro?" he yelled into the house. Nothing. He stepped into the doorway and his foot slipped. Something (*Jell-o?*) stuck to the side of his boot and refused to shake off. There was more of it in the entryway. It glistened and smelt like floodwater. Potter stepped back out of the house and walked around the side, scraping his foot in the grass as he went.

He still expected Mark to be out on the boat, at least two sheets to the wind, his phone on silent in his pocket. He expected it so much that when he saw Mark's legs on the ground, poking out through the cattails, and saw the boat bobbing empty out in the middle of the pond, he only rolled his eyes at his friend's intemperance. But that pit in his stomach grew significantly heavier.

"Mark? You forgot to . . . oh Jesus. Oh fuck fuck fuck. Mark. Jesus, what—" Potter vomited the pit in his stomach all over the cattails. Tully barked excitedly and sniffed at the barf, spinning around next to his dead master's feet, before looking up mournfully at Potter then forgetting the whole thing and yapping himself mad again.

Potter wiped his chin with his shirt. Mark lay at the water's edge, half in, half out. His head lolled back and forth as the water rippled against it. His eyes were wide and glazed and that jelly stuff from the doorway leaked from his mouth and globbed down his cheek. Something familiar tapped at the back of Potter's mind, but he couldn't focus for looking at Mark's throat. It bulged impossibly and bled from great deep furrow-like claw marks all along the sides of his Adam's apple that reached up over his cheeks like something had tried to dig its way in.

135

Potter half gagged, half sobbed, and pulled Mark by his boots up out of the water. He called 911 and their boss, then waited for the authorities to arrive. When his part was all done, he loaded Tully and a bag of dog food up in his car and drove home. He pulled in his driveway and lit up a cigarette, not caring about stinking up his "clean" truck. He supposed with Mark gone, he'd have to carry all the equipment anyway. He sat smoking for a long time, Tully asleep on the passenger seat and occasionally whimpering. He smoked and thought and tried to figure out what it was that looked familiar about that goo covering his friend's mouth. But all he could see was the way Mark's head bobbed in the water, and all he could remember was how much it looked like that big dead bullfrog he'd seen as a kid.

Potter woke, draped across the kitchen table with a glass still in his hand, to a ringing phone and a rat terrier licking his earlobe. Marianne. *Shit*, he thought. He hadn't even texted her.

"Marianne. I'm sorry . . ."

"Potter! Are you ok? I just heard. Oh my god."

"Yeah. I mean, no, but . . . I'll be ok." He stood and stooped over to pull down the window shade before the sun melted his aching eyeballs. "I'm sorry I didn't call."

"Oh honey, it's—it's fine. I just—what happened to him?"

"No fucking idea. Got drunk and slipped, I guess. It looked like he choked on his own puke. Something ate on him."

"So it happened again."

"Marianne. Jesus. Don't—"

"Don't '*don't*' me. You saw that and didn't even *think* about Clayton? They said they found Mark's own skin underneath his fingernails. That didn't even ring a bell?"

"Honestly, no, Marianne. I saw my best friend dead and I didn't think about your son, no."

The line was silent. Potter heard her drop something.

"I'm sorry."

"No, it's ok. I'm sorry. They're going to find something someday, though. Something that'll show everyone what happened to Clayton, that he didn't just drown, you know?"

"No, Marianne. They won't."

The rest of the conversation hadn't gone any better. It never did. But Potter had to give Marianne credit. She was a true believer. She never wavered, never stopped telling people that her son hadn't drowned. Five years ago, they'd found Clayton along the creek bank. His body was gray and cold, but it looked like he'd been sleeping, curled up on his side, his hands by his face. He looked like he was sleeping until you saw his eyes. Wide and bulging, like he'd seen something coming for him. After you saw his eyes, you might think his hands looked more like he'd been trying to ward something off.

The coroner said Clayton had drowned. They found him with his feet in the creek, after all. There were no cuts or bruises, so what else could it be? But Marianne knew that her boy was a strong swimmer. He waded the creek all the time, and the water wasn't even deep that summer. Then there was that business about them not finding any water in his lungs. But the death certificate had been signed, and Emmet County moved on. People didn't like thinking about a dead little boy any more than they needed to. People especially didn't like to think it was anything other than a child whose mother should have been paying closer attention to him.

Potter had been with Marianne through the whole thing. As much as he loved her, he was tired. Sometimes he thought he'd been tired since it happened. This morning, he was exhausted.

He poured some dog food on the floor for Tully and put his head in his hands.

Sometime later, hangover faded and head cleared, he and Tully drove back over to Mark's house. The front door had been closed and locked, but no one had thought to see to the truck. Potter pulled out the gigs and nets and smiled a little at how absolutely filthy everything was. *Dirty bastard*, he thought. *I can't forget you if I'm cleaning your muck out from under my nails for the rest of eternity.* He looked out back at Mark's pond as he loaded up his truck. The cattails waved, and the spring peepers started up their chorus. It wasn't even late afternoon and they were already going. The sound drilled into his eardrums. He turned up the radio as loud as he could stand and drove off to do yesterday's job.

Catching frogs was easy. He'd been doing it since he was a kid. Net. Harpoon gig. Bucket. Live and dead samples and back to the office to dump them out and analyze them. But today it was too easy. They were everywhere. Every step along the bank raised up a *chirp!* and two or three little frogs plopping into the water. He could reach down a gloved hand and scoop them up. Occasionally one would ribbit and bounce off his pant leg. Catching bullfrogs was usually moderately more difficult. There were fewer of them and they were better at hiding. Potter raised his eyes from his work and saw a dozen eyes glaring back at him.

"Fuck. *Off.*" He chucked a gig at the closest one.

"*JUGRUM!*" It leapt, too late, and the spear caught it right in the side.

"Serves you right." Potter retrieved the gig, shaking the frog, a big fat female, off the end. She landed with a wet *plop* and wriggled. Something wriggled. Potter leaned down to look. *Tadpoles.* Spilling out of her gashed-open belly. Not eggs, but tadpoles. But that was impossible. Frogs laid eggs. Females splooshed out a jelly-like clutch of eggs, males came along and jizzed on them, and soon you had tadpoles. Unless—Potter remembered a college textbook and a passage about some extinct frog in Australia that ate the fertilized eggs, protecting them in her wet belly until they hatched, then barfing up a few dozen wriggling tadpoles. *Gastric brooding.* A weird evolutionary answer to unfavorable environments, shrinking wetlands, and not enough safe places to hide her eggs. Potter felt his gorge, or maybe the leftover whiskey in his gut, rising again at the thought of it, and the thickness at the back of his throat made him think of Mark's bulging throat. *Gastric brooding,* he thought. *What a gross fucking phrase.* He spit on the wiggling puddle of tadpoles and left.

Potter turned his reports in at the office. Dumped the live samples off in the tanks. Used the department pressure-washer to clean off all the gear that he guessed was now his to haul around. He was just about to climb up into his truck and head for home when he saw Boss-man striding across the parking lot toward him.

"Hey buddy."

"Hey." Potter didn't look up.

"You coulda' taken the day off, you know."

"Work to be done."

"You doing ok?"

"Sure, I suppose." Neither man spoke. Boss-man looked like he wanted to give him a hug or something. "So what's up?"

"Oh, nothing. State boys just been calling a lot this week. Want to know about our counts. You got anything for them?"

"My reports are on your desk. Why's the state sniffing around?"

"Wish I could say. They keep asking about 'anomalies or irregularities.'"

Potter searched Boss-man's face. Live tadpoles spilling out of a frog's stomach was certainly an anomaly. "My reports are on your desk."

"Sounds good. Take care of yourself, Potter. Mark was a good man." Boss-man clapped him on the shoulder and started to look like he wanted a hug again. Potter left before it got any worse.

Marianne was waiting for him. She looked fantastic. She always did. He ached when he saw her in her long dress, leaning in his kitchen doorway, and wished, as he always did, that she'd move in with him. She never would, though. Always wanted to stay in her home. In her and Clayton's home. Everything in Marianne's house sat just like it had five years ago. Just like their relationship. Nothing was ever bad, but nothing ever changed. Potter wondered if she'd still dress up for him if they lived together anyway.

"Come here," she said, and he obeyed. She held him for a long, long time. Brushed her fingers through his hair. Kissed his neck and waited until the tension went out of his body. Then she led him out to the back deck where a big plate of meatloaf and mashed potatoes and two bottles of wine waited.

After they'd finished and he'd poured the last of the wine, they sat and talked. The frogs trilled relentlessly. Buzzing and peeping in the trees and on the deck all around them, but the wine had blunted the sharpness of the sound. Or maybe Potter was just getting used to it.

After a while, Marianne ventured, "So, what are they going to do about Mark?"

"I don't know. We're under a state hiring freeze. I don't think there's a my-partner-died exception. I guess I'll cover for him. It's just . . ."

"What?"

"I'm kind of starting to hate the water. What the fuck am I doing, anyway? I've been doing this job for half my life and I keep telling myself I'm protecting wetlands and promoting conservation, but all I'm doing is counting goddamned salamanders and mucking around in the mud. Nobody's listening to the numbers we're putting out anyway. The weather's getting worse. The water's getting worse. I was out at Norman's pond today and—I think the frogs are starting to hate me too."

Jugrum. Off in the distance.

"See! Damn bullfrog is cussing me."

Marianne laughed. "You haven't been away from the water for more than 24 hours since I've known you. You were just like Clayton. He was just like you. I couldn't keep that kid out of creeks and ponds for the life of me. Born with fins for feet, I used to say." She paused and took a deep breath. "I still miss him so bad, Potter."

"I know you do. So do I."

"He looked up to you just like you were his daddy."

"I wish I could have been."

JugRUM. Deeper now. Closer, too. *JUGRUM.* The bass reverberated in Potter's chest cavity, like he felt the croak rather than hearing it.

"Clayton used to love those real deep croakers," she said. "He'd always tell me, 'The deeper the sound, the bigger the frog.' He'd make his voice go real deep and have me try to guess how big the biggest frog out there was."

Juuuugrumm. It was almost subsonic. Potter tossed back the rest of his wine and went inside.

He woke in darkness. The wine was wearing off, but his brain still felt foggy. Marianne sighed in her sleep and shifted beside him. He was glad she was there next to him, and he reached out to brush her thigh, just to feel her warmth.

She moaned and rolled over. He lay still, hating to disturb her. When he dared to look, she was smiling sleepily at him. "Trying to cop a feel while I'm unconscious? That'll lose you a state job real quick."

"Shh, go back to—" he started, but she put a finger to his lips.

"*You* shh," she said, then slipped her finger in his mouth. She drew it out and painted it soft and wet over his lips. He sucked it back in hungrily. "Much better," she said. She teased her other hand down his chest, around and over his hips, touching everywhere but where he wanted. Then she drew her hand back under the covers, and after a quick wriggle, tossed her panties out of the bed. Potter had seen this trick a hundred times, but it never failed to impress. He rolled over to her, putting his hand on her shoulder to ease her on to her back. She resisted.

"No," she said, raising herself up onto an elbow and gently pushing him back onto the pillow. "Me."

Potter closed his eyes and smiled, anticipating the warm wetness that would soon envelop him. He raised his hips eagerly. But she didn't straddle his waist. He felt her knees on either side of his head as she positioned herself over his face.

Without opening his eyes, he lifted his chin and lapped. "There," Marianne whispered. "That's the spot." She lowered herself down onto his face and he licked and kissed. Slick sweetness. He was famished for her and she ground herself down onto him. He reached up and grabbed her thighs, pulling her closer against him and probing her with his tongue. Her wetness ran across his cheeks and over his chin. She was saying something, but he couldn't make out the words — her legs against his ears muffled the sound. He licked harder and she moaned, a deep, guttural sound. Then something slid past his lips. He tried to close his mouth, but his jaw was forced open, wide. Something was in his mouth, something big, pulsing, sliding down his throat. He felt tiny . . . *hands?* . . . tiny feet kicking for purchase against the inside of his cheeks, and he gagged and coughed, clawing at his face, clawing at his mouth, reaching in until he grabbed a leg and pulled as hard as he could. It was like vomiting an entire sausage. He flung it across the room, tears streaming from his eyes, and flicked on the bedside lamp.

Frogs. Everywhere. On the walls. In the bed. Potter threw back the covers and peeled off a toad that clung to his pubic hair. He screamed and jumped onto the floor, crushing slick bodies underneath his feet. Tiny bones splintered into his soles, and he slipped on their guts as he ran out of the room.

He was still naked in the kitchen, brushing imagined frogs from his legs when his phone rang on the counter. It was Marianne.

"Potter!"

"Marianne! Where are you?"

"I'm at home! It got late and I went home. Potter, the frogs! They're everywhere! What's happening?"

"I don't know. But just stay there."

"Hurry! They're hitting the windows!"

"Stay there! I'm coming to get you. Just stay there." He heard something like glass breaking and hung up the phone, grabbing his keys as he ran out the door. There were work pants in his truck, and he threw himself in the cab, pulling them on as he drove. He wondered dimly where Tully was. He hadn't seen the dog all night.

Rain pounded against the windshield. Small frogs caught in the wipers, and Potter couldn't tell if they'd jumped from the ground or fallen from the sky, but their guts smeared across the glass and made it impossible to see. There were thousands on the road. Their eyes glistened at him in the headlights. The pavement was slick with their flattened bodies. Potter kept the truck on the road until the last curve before Marianne's house. He should have slowed down, but she was so close. He turned to go around the curve, then jerked the wheel at the last second to avoid what he thought was a dog. Maybe even poor Tully. But it wasn't Tully. It was a bullfrog. Much bigger than a rat terrier. Even bigger than a beagle. Very much alive. Potter jerked the wheel and his tires fought for purchase and lost. The truck skidded to the side of the road, then turned over in a farmer's ditch.

Potter kicked out the broken side window and drug himself out. The rain coursed down, and the ditch was already starting to fill. Soon his truck would be underwater. But he couldn't worry about that now. He scrambled in the ditch, slipping in the mud and muck and sliding back down to the bottom where he landed on something large and soft and pink. A dead pig. It was a sow, a big pregnant one by the looks of it. Lightning flashed as Potter tried again to climb out of the ditch, and he should have known better but he looked back. The sow was heaving and twitching. *Oh my god, she's still alive.* But she wasn't alive, not by a long shot. Her great belly pitched and Potter heard himself screaming as a wave of wiggling tadpoles spilled out of her gullet.

He propelled himself up over the edge of the ditch and sprinted across the field, slipping every third step. He was a few hundred yards away from Marianne's front door when he slipped again and felt something tear in his groin. But his hands touched slick bodies and tiny clawed hands and he pushed himself on, limping until both hands were on her gate, like he was on base. Lightning flashed again, and the rain seemed to let up. He still heard mad croaking in the distance, but at least the house wasn't crawling in frogs.

"Marianne!" Potter burst through the door. The electricity was out. "Marianne!" A dim light flickered from underneath her bedroom door. *Oh thank God.* He rushed to her room and she lay in the bed, her back to him. His stomach sank, but then he heard her sigh and he nearly wept with relief. She turned towards him, eyes wide, as he wrapped his arms around her and pulled her tight to him.

"Oh Marianne. Oh thank Jesus. Come on, we've got to—"

She sighed again. But then Potter recoiled. Thick clots of jelly dripped from his arms. He stared, mouth agape, as a tiny tadpole squirmed from the corner of Marianne's mouth. It flopped onto the pillowcase. Her stomach contracted and a flood of tadpoles burst forth from between her lips. An impossible number. A seemingly endless tide of them spilled on the bedspread, on Potter's lap, all over the floor, until finally it stopped and one final, solitary bullfrog climbed up out of her throat and blinked at Potter. *Jugrum!*

People in Emmet County, Wisconsin still talk about that summer and the night with all the frogs. It was terrifying at the time, but as years pass, it becomes more of a tall tale and less of a memory. Sometimes one of the city newspapers will do a story on it at the anniversary, especially if it's been a very dry summer, or if people have been noticing a lot of frogs. Everyone remembers Marianne Woods' death, too, but over time, the two events have become less and less connected in people's minds. Her cause of death has never been determined, and no one really pushes on it. Everyone is happy enough to think that she and Clayton are finally reunited.

They don't know exactly what happened to Potter, either, though everyone has a pretty good idea. They found him at the Department of

Conservation office. He'd broken a window to get in. Reports and paperwork from the last decade were strewn all over the floor, and Potter lay in the middle of it all with a gig harpoon down his throat.

The summers in Emmet County get hotter every year. Every year the Department of Conservation sends their men out to do counts and surveys, and every year one or two black SUVs with tinted windows take away a few buckets of frogs. More livestock dies, and a few years ago, all of the pig farmers pulled up stakes and moved. But the corn thrives and the beans grow high, with hardly any bugs to worry them. It gets harder and harder to sleep at night, with all of the peeping and trilling, and every once in a while, a deep *JUGRUM!* will wake you and make you go around and make sure your windows and doors are sealed up tight.

CUTTERS

Victoria Day

I'D BEEN WORKING at the seafood farm for a few months before I knew something was wrong with the place. It may seem odd that a vegetarian should be working there but I have bills to pay and didn't fancy sofa surfing again. Besides, up here in the middle of nowhere there were few other opportunities for someone as young, unqualified, and unskilled as I was then. I reasoned with myself that I could try to do what I could to make the conditions better for the fish. Soon I would get enough money together to leave, move to the city and get a job at a café or in a supermarket. Dreams and university are for those who can afford it or who have a decent family. I had neither.

It seems to be a fact that many people don't even see fish or shellfish as animals. The amount of people who think vegetarians can still eat them! Just because they don't make noises and aren't cuddly or warm blooded doesn't mean they don't suffer. I've made it my goal to try to reverse that way of thinking. Fish do suffer, as I was to find out.

As I said, I'd been working at the fish farm, which was in a large warehouse type building with large tanks for the various types of sea life we harvested. I'd started working in the hatchery where the salmon eggs are hatched, so perhaps I wasn't fully aware of the cramped conditions they lived in until I started working where the tanks were. It was a bit of a disaster for the en-

149

vironment as well because of the sheer amount of waste they produced. But when did cruelty or eco damage ever get in the way of making money? It was a much cheaper way of providing fish than line fishing and that's all that seemed to matter to the owner. That owner was a man, Clive Bagby, whose grandfather and father had fished in the normal way as gamekeepers for the landed gentry. The tough and rugged life seemed to have made him determined to better his income and prospects. He'd obtained grants from the government and set up his first seafood farm. Judging by his car and clothes it was very profitable. I was one of a few young people from the local village who was taken on — at minimum wage — to do most of the actual work. He'd had a manager, a cousin called Ross Bagby who oversaw the farms, but from what I could gather there had been a somewhat mysterious falling out a few weeks before I started there, and he'd been sacked. I could never find out from the other workers exactly what had gone on between them.

One evening as I was returning to my digs in the village, I was hailed by an older worker, Jim, asking if I wanted to go with him and a few of the other workers for a drink. As all that awaited me was a cup of soup and a bit of leftover cake, I was in no hurry to get back to my tiny bedsit. We had an enjoyable evening as everyone was good for a bit of light-hearted chat, and it dawned on me that if I brought up the subject of Ross Bagby and why he'd been sacked, I might get some answers.

"He wasn't sacked, he left. Said he was fed up with Clive being a bossy bastard," said Jim.

"Nope. It was because he didn't like how the fish was being treated. Said it was cruel and that they were kept too close together," offered another man, Steve.

"Well, whatever it was made him go. He went and I don't think there was much love lost between 'em. Always hated each other I heard. Their grandfather, Len Bagby, now he was a good fella, but it was said that he left all his money to Clive's dad and none to Ross' dad. So, they fell out and so of course the lads fell out too."

"So why did Clive take Ross on then?" was my question. There was a chewing of lips, a few slurps of beer and a cough or two, and the answer finally came that Ross had had money problems, gambling and so on, and had come cap in hand to his cousin for a job.

"Caused a lot of bitterness I think," offered Jim, and the subject was changed to the football as it always was.

Work the next week was as uneventful as ever, but the week after that brought a bit of excitement. No one had set eyes on Ross for a long while after he'd left but then he was seen about the village again. We had an informer in HR in the shape of Jim's wife, Susan, and she'd heard that Ross had come to the office late at night to see Clive, that there had been an argument and shouting and that Ross had stormed out, cursing, and swearing. Why he'd come back and what he wanted, and presumably didn't get, she didn't know. "But, oh my what a face he had on him when he came out!" she said, looking worried.

The next week I was transferred from the hatcheries to the indoor tanks. Put out of your mind the image of an aquarium with various forms of sea life swimming peacefully about. These were little more than round, swimming pool-like tanks set deep into the concrete floor. The fish, snails and shellfish had no quality of life at all. It was the salmon I felt the worst about. They were packed in so tightly that they fought for space and some even became deformed. The tanks they were in also had edible sea snails in, to save space and therefore money. Added to that was the problem in all species of various kinds of parasites. Most of the creatures had some form of infestation which the workers tried to fight with chemical baths and removal of the worst affected creatures. We were told to keep quiet about the extent of the problem as Clive didn't want us to be shut down. I think I started hating him then. There were whispers around the place that the parasites were the reason for the bad feeling between Clive and Ross rather than the division of their grandfather's estate.

The salmon were afflicted by sea lice, tiny flat crustaceans with sharp mouth parts which ate away at the fishes' scales. When this happened death wouldn't be far off. They'd cling to the sides of the fish like brown blots and were difficult to get rid of. In the wild the salmon would swim to salt water which would get rid of them, but here, packed too tightly together, the things spread with appalling ease. The snails were prey to a type of microscopic grey worm which dissolved flesh and burrowed their way into the internal organs and grew there. One infected snail could spread them to a whole tank. When the snail died the worm, now fully grown and as long as a pencil, would curl out of the body and swim off to lay its eggs in another wretched snail. A lad called Paul and I had the misfortune to be given the job of sorting through the salmon and the snails, looking for these parasites and trying to get rid of them. The sea lice removal involved getting hold of a fish by its tail, a smelly and exhausting feat, and then picking the lice off with a blunt knife. Other farms had proper treatment systems but they cost too much money of course. I hated it when I caught the fish's skin and damaged their iridescent scales. I could feel through my hands and arms the poor fish's floundering and panic as it nearly drowned in air. It was as if I were being nearly murdered as well. Most other workers didn't see it that way, but probably would have been horrified if asked to do something similar to a mammal. The snail parasite removal was even more unpleasant. This involved taking hold of a snail and checking under its shell for any small holes. We weren't looking for the tiny, juvenile versions of the parasites, but the adult ones emerging from their soft grey flesh. As far as Clive was concerned, selling suffering and infected animals to eat wasn't a problem. I hoped that Ross might confront him and put a stop to it. If not, I knew that I would have to. But the next month something awful happened.

We were detailed to do another parasite removal stint on the salmon and snail tank. When we did this, we threw the parasites into a large shallow container which was emptied at intervals into a furnace. We were meant to wear thin latex gloves, but these were too slippery to be of any use, so we just used our bare hands. The worms from the snails we got hold of by their heads. We then had to wind them up onto a type of long needle and flick them into the shallow container. We'd done this a few times before, but as soon as we started I could sense that something was different. The salmon seemed even more listless than usual and quite a few were dead and floating on top of the water. I pointed this out to Paul, and he got a scoop to remove them.

"Christ!" He shouted, dropping the scoop onto the floor. The fish flicked and jerked, but they were dead. The reason they moved was soon seen; dozens of worms attached like suckers to their underbellies twitched and shook. Others were fixed around the head of the fish, their thin bodies writhing as they slid into its gaping mouth. Some had already got into its gills which bled. Paul stamped on them with disgust and spat out, "Shit, let's get this done. God knows what those little bastards are. Look, this one's got a face. Bloody pincers on it."

"Can't be the snail worms, they don't have those mouth parts."

"Fuck knows, come on. There's only those few fish dead. The rest look ok. Hmm, no sea lice on 'em, that chemical bath Jon did must have worked."

We carried on, working for a good few hours. It was true that no sea lice could be found, which was a relief, so we just worked on the snails who were badly affected with the worms, some having several large holes in them with adult worms emerging. These seemed to know what we were up to and when we had them by the head they would move with a blind, nosing motion and then, with a horrible appearance of intelligence they'd stop and lurch towards us. A few times I only just managed to get my hand away. A few did seem to have an appearance of sharp pincers, so I was glad about that. After this had happened again and again, I joked that the things had evolved since last month and were out to get us. He laughed but stopped abruptly when there was a surging movement in the pile of worms in the container.

It was as if a wave rose up out of a calm sea.

A wave with a low humming sound.

A wave which looked at us.

With a shout of "Christ! Look at that!" Paul went closer and leaned over the container. Whether he slipped or was so shocked by what he saw that he felt faint and fell in, we never did find out, but the next thing was that he fell into the container. We managed to pull him out, but his face was covered with dozens of the things. They moved in a way that made me feel sick, spreading down into his collar. Some moved towards his hair, the mass shifted slightly and for a moment we were presented with the horrific sight of worms burrowing in under his left eyelid and into his tear ducts. Others curled like acrobats over his lips. If it didn't sound impossible, I'd have said that they moved like a small, deadly army, with purpose and coordination. He screamed over and over then started spitting and coughing. Others ran over and we washed his face and made him rinse his mouth out with fresh water. He was a tough sort of guy who didn't like to show weakness or fear and soon brushed off any suggestion that he see a doctor or go home.

We were told of his death after a phone call to the office from the sister with whom he lived. Clive didn't bother to tell us of course; it came from one of the older foremen. Apparently, he'd gone home and taken a hot bath but hadn't been able to eat any dinner. All he'd had was about half a bottle of whisky which he'd told his sister was to "drown the little bastards" in his throat. He'd complained about pain there and in his chest, but again had refused to see a doctor. His sister had been woken in the night with a terrible noise of him making a strangled, gurgling sound. She'd rushed in to find him being sick and coughing up what she took to be bloody flesh. She rang for an ambulance, but before it arrived, he'd died, still gasping and pulling over and over at his throat. He'd looked, she said, as if he were trying to get something out from inside his mouth and his hands were coming away covered in blood and phlegm.

As you can imagine, we were shocked as well as grieved at this, and although there were half hearted mutterings about Paul's drinking, the possibilities of the flu or a strep throat and so on, we all knew that it was those parasites in the container which had got down his throat. It was especially puzzling as we knew that these parasites didn't normally try to live in or on humans, much less actually attack them. We'd seen them latch onto his face, though, and were frightened by the idea that they'd gone for him on purpose. What scared us more, though, was the disappearance of the container the parasites had been in. Kev, the man whose job it was to tip it into the furnace, denied doing so and so did everyone else. Both container and parasites had vanished.

The next day the Health and Safety people, advised by the police, closed the farm down pending inquiries. An autopsy was ordered on Paul and the result of that caused a fair bit of surprise among his fellow workers, although Clive seemed pleased. The pathologist said that death could not be due to parasites as that was not the way they acted. They didn't attack humans and their aim was to feed from a host and not to kill it immediately. There was substantial damage to

Paul's throat and also to his lungs, and it was the pathologist's opinion that he must have swallowed and inhaled some of the parasites which had then caused an infection. Some live parasites were found inside the back of his throat and in the tops of his lungs. He did, however, admit that the whole thing was unusual. It was peculiar that his tongue was so badly damaged underneath, but this was put down to being the result of violent retching.

Quite a few of us suspected that Clive had put pressure on the Chief Constable, who was an old friend, so that a more palatable reason for Paul's death could be found. But it satisfied none of his friends and certainly not his sister. I overheard talk in the pub that she had heard not only Paul's retching and cries, but also a noise she didn't recognise. She'd described it as a murmur with a clicking sound mixed in. It had become louder until poor Paul's final scream had blotted the noise out. When they'd asked her what had happened to the bloody mess he'd coughed up, she'd become distressed and said that most had been vomited down the toilet, but some had gone on the bathroom floor. It had been moving, she said.

The fate of the farm hung in the balance. A few of us met in the village pub to talk about it, as many of us were concerned for our future; the rumour was that the place might reopen if certain measures were put into place. Health and Safety for staff had to be improved, as you'd expect, but also the livestock's welfare, fewer animals in each tank, better measures for their quality of life and so on. Parasite prevention didn't seem to be a concern which caused a good deal of anger amongst the other employees as well as puzzlement. It was thought, possibly with justification, that Clive had friends in high places. One of the angriest was Ross, who came one night to the pub, bought a few rounds and talked, or rather ranted, about how he felt. Clive was, he said, a man who was only concerned with making money and didn't care how he made it. Did we know he'd been cutting corners for years at the farm? That our wages were considerably less than at farms in other countries? That the stock on the farm ought to have been destroyed and new brought in because of the parasite infections, but that Clive knew a thing or two about the bloke from the Ministry who had underplayed the extent of the problem.

Clive's only aim now was to get his cursed farm up and running and he (Ross) knew damn fine it would be just as bad as before. There had been similar incidents in the past, admittedly not ending in a death, and they'd been covered up. At first, we listened with a good deal of sympathy, but as he got steadily more drunk, and his comments became more violent against his cousin, we became uncomfortable and perhaps a little frightened. Ross went on, saying that Clive had tricked him out of their grandfather's inheritance as he'd lied to the grandfather when he was dying, telling him that Ross's dad couldn't be bothered to go to see him, but all the time he'd been hiding how ill the old man was. He'd always been a sneaking little bastard and he hated him. He'd murdered Paul because of his bloody meanness. After this last comment, Ross seemed to recollect where he was and realised that we were all staring at him. He looked embarrassed, laughed uneasily and left the pub. Of course, when he'd gone, we enjoyed a good long discussion of what he'd let slip. We'd heard of his antipathy to Clive but hadn't actually seen it.

The weeks went by while the farm was still shut up. The rumours about what the Ministry and Health and Safety would be likely to recommend continued and we were pleased that the issue of the parasites in the livestock might be addressed after all. This was according to one of Clive's secretary's brother who worked in the minimart in the village. His sister had let slip that there had been several phone calls to Clive about this very matter and that he had been heard alternately shouting and pleading down the phone, possibly trying to force the Ministry to accept his suggested measures. This was all conjecture and none of us really knew what was going on. The local press had got hold of the story and attempted to get Clive's view, but he'd given out an official "no comment" which of course set rumour flying in all directions. Many of us could hold on no further with no money coming in — Clive had only paid us a month's wages — and quite a few got jobs away from the village in the next large town. This was helped by the local council deciding, not a moment too soon in the opinion of most villagers, to provide a more regular bus service between the village and town. I still had a few months to run on my rent and my digs and being short of money decided to stay on in the village for the foreseeable future. The secretary's brother went back to university in the city, and I took over his job at the minimart. It was pretty boring, but at least it was cleaner and a lot less horrible than the farm. Besides, I was starting to have nightmares about Paul's accident and imagining his terrible death. After the first few weeks the farm was still shut up, and one morning at work Clive appeared at the minimart.

"You free?" he whispered to me after he popped up behind me.

"Yeah, I can ask the boss for five minutes. What do you want?"

"Out here."

We went out through the back door, something never usually allowed by Cheryl, my boss, but it was Clive, and he did as he liked. By the bins and squashed down cardboard boxes he leant against the wall and lit a cigarette, not offering me one.

"You were the one who was with Paul when he had his accident. I can't remember your name."

"It's—"

"When he had his accident. And it was an accident, wasn't it?"

His tone and the way he looked at me through the cigarette haze implied that I had better agree with him. His eyes looked red and puffy, and his breath was ripe with the smell of whisky.

"No. You know what happened. Ross knows too."

"Sod him. It was an accident and when the Ministry come, asking around, you had better agree with me. I know what happened to your parents and you'd do well to make sure it doesn't happen to you. They'll shut me down for good this time. So, when the nice man comes round asking questions, you tell him you and Paul were checking the stock and that Paul fell in a tank of snails and a few must have got swallowed. OK?"

I didn't have the chance to respond. He was off again, leaving his half-smoked cigarette on the ground dangerously close to the cardboard boxes. I stamped it out and fell back against the filthy wall, my heart going like a broken clock and struggling for my breath. How did he know about my parents?

The Ministry team came to the village the week after this. I had been too frightened to say anything about my run-in with Clive to anyone. I toyed with the idea of telling Ross, but worried that he'd just stamp straight over to Clive's office and challenge him with what I'd said. I was still anxious about what Clive had said about my parents and don't forget that I was young, poor and had no family to back me up. I thought to myself that as soon as this is sorted out and I have a few hundred quid, I'm getting out of here. The farm was still shut up of course, with no one allowed in except to feed the stock and clean the tanks. Although the Ministry apparently gave no credence to the parasites being the direct cause of Paul's death, the workers they sent in wore industrial level protective gear and breathing apparatus. Presumably then there were still parasites living on the bodies of the poor creatures. As they were from the Ministry, we didn't get any gossip about what it was like in there or if the tank of parasites which Paul had fallen into had been found. I wondered if they even knew about the circumstances of his death. Perhaps they hadn't been told.

Despite all this the order came through after a week that the stock had to be destroyed. I know that they were only snails and fish, and their fate would have been death anyway, but I felt awful about it. Some news had leaked out eventually, despite the Ministry's attempts at secrecy. Nearly all the fish and snails were riddled with parasites and several kinds of chemicals used at the farm were either illegal or too corrosive. The whole farm was declared a biohazard and was closed up. As the news of this development spread through the village there was a good deal of anger, as people wondered what might have been dumped into the sea or the river and how that might affect their water supplies and the local wildlife. Clive might have found his tyres slashed and a few bricks through his windows.

But Clive had disappeared.

He'd been reported missing by his wife after she'd not seen him for a couple of days. It seemed that Clive had a few, let's say extracurricular interests, which took him off for days at a time. His wife had eventually taken the step of ringing the lady in question and she hadn't seen him for days either. The police were informed but they and the locals seemed to think he'd cleared off to hide for a while, especially as it was discovered that a good deal of cash had been drawn out of the business account, put in the office safe and was now missing. Ross was still seen about the village, but he seemed to know no more than anyone else and there was no more family to ask. I'd finally managed to get a place at the college in the nearest city, student digs and a job in a coffee and book shop there so my interest in the fish farm waned a bit. I might never have returned to the village except to see a few old workmates, until I realised that the only photo I had of my parents was missing.

I went back to my old digs to see if it had fallen behind the gas fire or if it had been found by my landlady, but then I remembered that one day I'd taken it to show poor Paul and had stuck it in the inside of the door of my locker. I had to get it back, even though that meant getting into the sealed-up farm building. One moonless night I arrived late at the village and managed to get through the outer fence and in through a nailed up wooden office door which had already been prised off its hinges and replaced. At first, I thought it must have been kids, but when I put it back in place I saw that a plank of wood had been nailed to the inside of its frame to hold it in place. Possibly this had been done by the Ministry people, but it looked too makeshift for that. I moved though the office which had a little light from the distant streetlights. Then I went into the corridor, then into the tank room, and onto one of the metal gantries above the tanks. It was utterly black, and I didn't dare turn on a light. The first thing that hit me, worse in the dark, was the appalling smell. It had always been pretty awful in there but now the smell was like a solid mass. Most tanks had been emptied of life and water by the Ministry, so where was the stench coming from? I soon got my answer. I felt my way about in the blackness toward the door to the staff room, trying not to breathe, and my lower body smacked right into the source of it. It was the missing tank of parasites that Paul and I had used on that awful day. It had been half full then, but now it was up to the brim and my head nearly went into it. I panicked and gagged, stepping backwards. Straight into Ross. The lights came on, filling my eyes with too much brightness. I saw more than the desolate tank room. I saw Ross, smiling at me, and I saw Clive.

At first, I didn't even realise that the mess on the floor was human. It was humped over on all fours and was completely silent. Then a revolting noise, like a retching, scratching moan started up. I saw a signet ring on one of the fingers which weren't ragged and bloody and recognised the thing as Clive. I managed to speak.

"Ross, what the fuck's going on? Did you find him here? How long's he been here?"

"I got him here with the only thing he's been interested in. Money. I broke into the safe and took his runaway funds. Told him he could collect it here and I'd say nothing. I needed something to experiment with to see what else the parasites could do." Ross came up close to me and looked into my eyes. He laughed, but not the jolly laugh I was used to hearing from him. It was mean and more like a shallow intake of air. He pointed at the parasite tank.

"Come and look. I took them away that day poor old Paul fell in them. Clive here made them and then wanted to kill them."

"Made them? What . . . ?"

"Those snail worms and sea lice can crossbreed, did you know that? That's why they aren't meant to be kept together, but Clive knew best, and it brought more money in. They'd been doing that for years here, only no one noticed. You did though, didn't you? Have a look, they've changed even since you saw them. A miracle of evolution!"

I edged to the tank and looked in. There were thousands of them. Worms. Now brown-grey and smaller like the sea lice and each with their crab-like flesh cutting mouths.

"That's why your pal Paul died so quickly. They weren't as far along as these beauties, but they already started to bite and could still dissolve flesh. Got in his lungs and his throat, poor bastard. Ate him. I took them home in my van.

Been interested in these things for ages. I could tell what would happen but of course Clive didn't give a toss. He does now."

He fixed a hand on my neck, which felt like a pincer itself, and pushed me down towards Clive's face. With his other hand he forced open Clive's mouth.

"Open up, Clive. Show your lying little mouth."

Inside what had been a jaw was now just a shredded, wet mess of bone and blood, phlegm and what looked like vomit.

"Clive's got no tongue to tell his tales with now. It's been dissolved and eaten. I call them Cutters."

He let me go and stepped back and looked at me as if he expected a round of applause.

"Ross, you really need to get Clive some help. He needs the hospital. You can't want him to die."

Ross was above one of the half-filled tanks and managed to say, "Oh yes, but I do indeed!" when Clive must have found a last bit of strength. He rose up as far as he could, blood dripping from his face, clasped his ruined arms around Ross's body and fell with him from the gantry down into the tank. At first there was silence, then a chattering, scraping sound like I'd heard when the parasites had attacked Paul. I heard Ross scream and a blood-wet, airless laugh came from Clive.

I ran.

THE TEMPLE OF THE SPIDER GOD

Steven Savile

"THEY WORSHIP SPIDERS, don't they?"

"Primitive culture, Gilroy. They'd worship a shoe if you presented it to them and said it was magical."

"Ah, right, of course, just like the politicians back home."

Gilroy Sinclair threw his head back, but didn't actually laugh. It was a strange affectation, feigning amusement. But it was very much Gilroy Sinclair. The man had been born in the damned pits of the North and came out covered in coal dust, but spoke as though a silver spoon had been stuck up his backside ever since. Solid silver, too, none of that cheap plating for Gilroy Sinclair.

Beneath the pith helmet his flowing blond locks were matted with a glue of sweat that left him looking far from divine.

To be fair, none of the locals would mistake either of them for gods, no matter how primitive they were. Devils, maybe . . . ghouls, almost certainly.

When they'd set out upon their grand adventure neither of the men had considered that sweat might be the great leveller. Sweat, of all things. But it was one thing for some well-meaning bag man to remind them that the temperatures in this hellhole of a land were consistently beyond even the hottest days back home, and quite something else to slog through the bizarre climates of the rainforest for several weeks, losing weight by the hour as the sweat quite literally diminished them.

With the drinking water in their canteens preciously close to dried up, and more pounds and ounces sweated out into the fabric of their clothing, the sensible thing would have been to admit defeat, give up the search for the temple of the Spider God, turn tail and go home. But Gilroy Sinclair and Malcolm Faraday were a lot of things, and sensible wasn't a word that found its way into either man's vocabulary, especially when a grand journey was on the cards. This was all about the spirit of adventure. And, to be fair, how could they resist the challenge Lockhart had thrown down? Bring home the Spider God in a jar and they'd get his Bayswater Road house, so sure was the blowhard that there was no such temple, and Faraday and Sinclair were gullible fools for believing the legends that fake fakir had spun them, but better by far than bricks and mortar, they'd humiliate the man in front of everyone from the Blackfriars Club, and *that* was a reward beyond price.

The pair had left London full of the vim and vigour of righteous indignation, determined to see Lockhart eat his words. The thought of that sustained them through the darkest days of the journey, long after it had ceased to be an adventure. The tramp steamer they'd chartered from Chatham had taken them so far, then contacts in Orungu ensured they had bag men to carry their burdens as they ventured into the forests. Orungu had been a most peculiar place. Its entire existence was predicated on ivory, beeswax, dyewood, copal and ebony. But the times were changing. The place was teeming with brokers still, but they weren't trading wax or wood, they were trading souls, their only crimes being to displease the self-styled Chief of the tribes.

They weren't here to change the world, merely to win a wager, so when it came down to moral choices, the pair were more than happy to take half a dozen of the tribesmen into their employ and set off into the rainforest in pursuit of the legendary Spider God.

The problems came when they ventured deeper into the rainforest, ignoring the markers their bag men kept pointing out with nothing short of superstitious dread. Sinclair had seen them first; carvings in the tree trunks. All manner of spiders had been scratched into the bark. The men had recognised those markings, and refused to cross the lines they marked, heeding the warnings. But not the Englishmen. With tensions mounting between them, Ngumbo, who turned spokesman for the tribesmen as he was the only one with any command of the language, pointed out the reality of the situation: they were days into the dense rainforest, miles from any form of civilsation, and outnumbered six to two. No one was going to come to their rescue. "Do you really want to make a fight of this? You will lose and who will question us if we return without you? I will tell you. No one. They will simply assume the forest was too much for you, as it is for so many of you white skins. You turn up looking to conquer her, only to burn up and turn to dust to feed the land. That is the way it is."

"Quite the way with words you've got there, Ngumbo," Faraday muttered, but notably didn't try to force the issue, but instead offered a compromise. "How about we sit, break our fast, and instead you tell us some stories of these people and what these markings mean? We are eager to learn, aren't we Gilroy?"

"I am an empty vessel waiting to be filled with your knowledge."

They found fallen logs that would work as chairs, while the bag men were left to sit cross-legged on the ground, and unwrapped the wax-paper from what little remained of their precious victuals, sharing a few bites before they wrapped them up once more. The rations wouldn't last long. What neither man was prepared to admit was that they'd ventured long past the point of no return; even if they turned back now they would run out of food long before they were clear of the trees and back in the dubious safety of Orungu. Stuffing the wax-papered wrap back inside their belongings, Faraday commanded, "Well, entertain us."

Ngumbo scratched out a symbol in the dirt by his feet. "You see this?" The man asked, earning nods from both men.

"On several trees," Gilroy agreed.

"It is the mark of Nsembelo, the one you call the Spider God. These are her lands. She nourishes them. She protects them. She is the land—"

"Where do we find this Nsembelo?"

"—You do not. Not in the way that you want. All you will find, should you be unlucky enough to stumble upon her, is death."

"Might have been helpful if someone had said something a couple of weeks back, before we left the township," Gilroy Sinclair muttered, far from impressed with the native's fears. "But we're here now, so what say we risk it?"

"You are an arrogant man, Master Sinclair, and a fool, but I have no wish to see you in the dirt, so I urge you to reconsider this. Nsembelo was here long before the first man, making her home in this place. Every root and every branch is a part of her, growing out of her corpse even as they leech nourishment from the land to sustain her. She is the land and the land is her."

"And you know this because?"

"I have seen her. Once. As a boy."

"Ah, and you lived to tell the tale? Good. This is good. A little caution is wise, but there is no need for this fear in your head, man. Pull yourself together."

The bag man did not seem to understand the order, and took it in a more literal sense than Gilroy Sinclair had intended, wrapping his arms around his midriff and seeming to hug himself, hard. It would have been comical, but for the words coming out of his mouth now, like a rambling prayer.

"In our tongue she is more fittingly called the Spider Queen."

"Demoted from the divine? Quite the come down."

Ngumbu didn't react to the slight, "She is long dead, and gods do not die."

"So she was never a god? That's quite disappointing, isn't it, Gilroy?"

"How ever will we cope?"

This time, the local bristled at the tone, knowing when he was being mocked even if he didn't know the full subtleties of their words. It was a mistake to take the man for a fool simply because he wasn't born in St. Bartholomew's and didn't attend mass at St Martin's in the Field.

"Men like you have been coming for her for as long as there has been breath in the rainforest's lungs. You come, you seek to steal from her whatever it is that makes her magical . . . I am offering you the chance you do not deserve and would not offer me in your place. Turn around. Go home. This is no place for your kind. You are not welcome here. "

"We will not be intimidated or bullied out of our grand adventure, slave. You underestimate us. We are Englishmen. There is not a corner of this world that is not ours to command. There is not a creature on this earth that does not bow its head to our mastery. We shall not be cowed by stories of a dead woman, Ngumbo. We are not cowards. We are Englishmen. And you need to know your place. When we tell you to take us to this temple of your dead god, you will damned well take us to this temple, not try to frighten us with your superstitious claptrap, understood?"

"It is your funeral, *master*," Ngumbo said. "I will show you the way, but I will not set foot within that temple again. Once was enough. I have no wish to see her again."

"You are more than welcome to wait outside if you are afraid of the dark."

The black man smiled a smile of low cunning. Faraday did not like it. There was something disagreeable about the local. It was painfully obvious he resented their presence in his land. That made him an untrustworthy guide. But what choice did they have but to follow him deeper into this hellscape of trees and mist and rarefied air?

"You see this?" Ngumbo's finger traced two of the legs of the spider mark he'd scratched out in the dirt.

"Legs," Gilroy Sinclair muttered, fed up with the whole performance.

The guide's lips twitched in a smile. "I can see you are very fine Englishmen," he said, causing Faraday to bristle. "Well educated and with great minds. Spiders do indeed have legs, as you say. But look again."

Faraday saw it then, the mark had too many legs for it to be an arachnid. Curious. "Too many legs," he noted, causing his companion to say, "Primitive culture, Gilroy, who is to say they can even count?"

"Me," Ngumbo said. "There are two of you and six of us. That is counting, is it not?"

"Fine, so, tell me then, what is the significance of these extra legs? Enlighten me."

"They are not legs. But you will see for yourself soon enough, master. The temple is not far from here. Less than a day's walk. We will take you there."

"Finally," Gilroy Sinclair muttered. "Now we're getting somewhere. Come on then, man, time's a wasting." He was on his feet and ready to go. Faraday was slower to rise. Something about this did not feel right, but he followed the others deeper into the ancient woodland, aware of every little sound around them. The caws of the parrots and the sunbirds, the babbler and the paradise catcher. The rustle of the leaves as moisture that gathered in the higher canopy turned to a curious inner-forest rain, and fell in a ragged spatter, playing the thicker leaves of the lower canopy like drumskins. And other noises. Deeper noises. Hidden within the shadows. The rustle and bustle of predators following their prey.

Time and again, he reminded himself these creatures were more afraid of him than he was of them, and patted the rifle slung over his shoulder as though it had the stopping power to put down a rampaging elephant, or stop a big cat in its tracks.

They walked on, following their guides.

Faraday marked more and more of the curious carvings in the tree trunks, and quickly came to realise that they seemed to be growing more and more elaborate, which he took to mean they were getting closer to the lost temple, and their goal, the tomb of the dead Spider God.

What he wouldn't give to see Lockhart's face when they returned to the club with a vial containing the venom of the Spider God and put it down on the table in front of him. That would wipe the grin off the old Gammon's mug. It would almost be worth all of the discomfort they'd endured.

Scratch that. As their guide pushed back the undergrowth and they saw the moss-covered stones of a building set into the heart of the earth itself, he knew there was no almost about it. Faraday stumbled through the break in the thick vegetation, his foot snagging on a protruding root. As he pitched forward, Ngumbo's hand snaked out and caught his collar, stopping him from falling. The man's grip was vice-like. The button of his shirt damned near choked Faraday as it dug into his throat, but Ngumbo wasn't letting go.

He dusted himself off, but didn't thank the man.

In the distance he heard the raging rush of a river, the churn of the water rushing to find the sea.

Uncapping the water bottle from his hip, Faraday took a deep swig, and wiped the moisture from his lips with the back of his hand before he capped the bottle and set it back in place. The water was warm and thick going down, and under normal circumstances would have been far from pleasant, but right here, in this place, right now, in this time, it was a bleedin' elixir.

The clearing was half in shadow, and half a furnace, with the sun beating down on the anvil of the earth. Curiously, given the sheer heat, the vegetation remained a lush green, offering no hint that the fire of the sun had the power to sear it. And yet when Faraday looked at his companion, Gilroy Sinclair's skin was a rich rosy pink of pork crackling, sweat dripping like fat down his neck.

The temple rose up out of the ground, twin columns either side of a gaping wound of an entrance that descended deep into the darkness. Tangles of vine and moss clung to the pitted stone. It was hard to imagine how such a building could have been built in a place like this. Each of those stone blocks would have needed a small army to manoeuvre into place, never mind lift them.

"We go no further," Ngumbo said, speaking for the five bag men who had moved to stand behind him.

"That's fine, just watch the luggage, we shan't be long."

"And if you don't return?"

"There's nothing down there to be frightened of, man. You'll see."

"We will wait here. We are not worthy of encountering our gods. We know this."

"Suit yourselves."

And so saying, Gilroy Sinclair marched off towards the black wound in the world, and descended, Faraday struggling to keep up.

"I have no time for cowards," the explorer said, reaching for a faggot of wood that appeared to have been dipped in some sort of resin or oil. "I mean, how scary can this place be? They've gone to the effort of preparing torches!" Shaking his head, Gilroy brought forth flame, and there was light.

Not that Faraday particularly wanted light, as that meant seeing deeper into the darkness as they descended.

"What a peculiar place this is, old man."

There was no denying that.

They had gone no more than a dozen paces into the claustrophobic passage, and already the light of the real world was denied them, falling short of their feet. The only thing between them and absolute night was the guttering torch Gilroy held high. The flame revealed the lost world of the Spider God, which, in truth was nowt more than a narrow passageway and stones dripping with a peculiar ichor. It wasn't the stuff of immortal deities. It wasn't even worthy of a barrow boy on the South Bank. The sounds of their footsteps echoed back to them eerily.

"Can't say as I like it much," Faraday muttered.

He trailed his fingertips across the wall, expecting to feel dampness, but despite the sheen of what he'd taken to be moisture, the stone was bone dry. It was disconcerting to say the least. But he said nothing, unwilling to draw Gilroy's scorn.

The stone slabs beneath their feet sloped downwards. It was a gradual descent, but when he turned back to look the way they had come Faraday needed to lift his head to see the slice of sunlight that was the temple's entrance. The passage ahead of them twisted, doubling back even as it descended deeper. There were any number of such turns, making it impossible for the men to get their bearings in the cloying dark. The chill bristled across his skin, a portent of what was waiting for them around the next ramp.

And still they descended.

In the distance, the steady drip of water chimed, counting out the seconds of life left to them.

A breeze caused the flame to gutter, and the shadows to dance; Faraday felt it brush across his skin, but couldn't begin to explain how a wind might stir underground.

The walls were covered with all manner of iconography, he noted, though the significance of them was beyond him. They might just as easily have been neanderthal cave paintings for all the sense he made of them. There was no mistaking the spider at their heart, though, nor the fact that the artists had endowed the arachnid with too many legs, two of which it used more akin to mandibles to hold its prey as it cracked open its skull to suckle at the brains inside. It was not a pretty picture. Gilroy saw it, but said nothing about the art.

"Ignore it," the man up front said, as though reading Faraday's mind. "Primitive culture," he repeated. It was his mantra whenever faced with something he couldn't explain away or didn't understand. But Faraday was coming to realise there was a world of difference between a so-called primitive culture, and a different world, and this was very much the latter. There were different rules down here, in the dark.

And then he heard it, and damned as he was, he knew exactly what the slow rasping sound was—because it could only ever be one thing.

Breathing.

But what manner of thing could breath so loudly each exhalation could be heard dozens upon dozens of feet away from the mouth breather? It had to be a trick of the acoustics of the temple, surely, because if it wasn't this so-called Spider God had to be enormous. And then his mind was gone, chasing idle thoughts. In them he saw a spider the size of Big Ben back home, and tried to imagine the poor bastards labouring to build this temple over its bones, and rather than laugh it off, the thought sent a chill shiver down the ladder of Faraday's spine. He caught himself looking back over his shoulder, but there was no inviting light back there now, only the endless night of this pit. His heartbeat quickened. His own breathing came as counterpoint to the deeper menace of the breathing in the darkness ahead. It was all he could do to force himself to take another step forward, focussing intently on the guttering flame, even as the thought that it might somehow be the monstrous breathing that caused the flame to shiver.

He'd never considered himself to be a man afraid of the dark, but even at his age he could learn something new about himself, it would seem.

Up ahead, the light of the flame revealed a huge arch, and within, a chamber.

This was the heart of the tomb.

He had expected some sort of door to keep trespassers out, but there was nothing of the sort. It was almost as though the Spider God wanted to lure the unsuspecting into its lair. Even as the thought took root in Faraday's mind, he felt something brush against his face. He recoiled from the strange touch. Reaching up, he felt the strands of spider's web stick to his fingers. He caught himself before he could start laughing; there was nothing funny about the thickness of those strands of web between his fingers and any sound that slipped between his lips now would be nothing short of hysterical.

He wanted to close his eyes, but couldn't take them off what looked to be a writhing mass of roots and bugs that dominated the centre of the chamber.

"So much for a Spider God," while Gilroy sounded disappointed, Faraday was anything but. He followed the light as it revealed more contours to the shape, even if it made no sense to his mind. There was endless movement . . . life . . . as hundreds upon hundreds of thin legged and fat bodied spiders scurried away from the light. Thousands upon thousands. They had made their home within the mound, burrowing into the darker places within for shelter and nourishment.

Faraday couldn't pull his gaze away from the arachnids.

Some, he saw, were as large as his hand, and bore peculiar markings across their furred backs. Some had fangs that were more than a match for any of the predators they had seen out in the rainforest. It wasn't hard to imagine poison dripping down their length, nor what a bite might do to a man's flesh.

He knelt, holding out a hand to allow one of the smaller spiders to crawl across his palm. "Not sure how we're going to convince Lockhart to give up his townhouse with this chap, are you?" Gilroy said, that disappointment festering.

"Don't," Faraday said, but it was too late. Gilroy had already closed his fist, crushing the spider inside it. He wasn't sure what he'd expected—or feared—but the others didn't suddenly come swarming out of the mound looking to avenge their fallen comrade.

Gilroy just laughed at his nervousness.

"What a strange place this is . . ." he mused, venturing deeper into the chamber.

Gilroy crouched beside the mound, and as the flame lit it fully, Faraday realised what he was looking at. The mound was the huge abdomen of an even huger spider, and all of the smaller spiders they saw scurrying away from their light had made their homes within it. He couldn't even begin to imagine how many fed off the corpse. It was hard enough to accept that each bristle he saw was as thick as a finger, and that what he'd taken to be joists supporting the stone walls at first sight could only be legs, and where he'd thought the bloated white roots pushing up through the ground were from the rainforest forcing its way into this sacred chamber, now he began to understand he'd got it wrong and that the roots were growths coming out of the Spider God and pushing down into the earth to spread out far beyond the influence of this chamber, nourishing a huge swathe of the rainforest, its influence spreading from root to root, tree to tree.

And that, he realised sickly, was the true meaning of those warnings carved into the trees out there. They weren't to ward folk off at all, they were a lure.

"Come here, man, I want to get a closer look at this thing . . . it's . . . fascinating."

So saying, Gilroy stepped up to the side of the immense abdomen, and rested his free hand on the coarse furred skin, feeling the thrill of the Spider God breathing beneath his touch.

"Incredible," he breathed. "It's alive. It's alive!"

It took a moment for Faraday's brain to process what he was seeing, but he quickly realised that the seething movement across the bulbous abdomen wasn't due to the spiders crawling all over it, but from something pulsing within, like the skin was going to tear and millions more of the critters were going to come spilling out.

He caught himself breathing faster. Clenching and unclenching his fist. He wanted nothing more than to run, there was no fight reflex, purely flight. But he couldn't move his feet. Faraday was rooted to the spot every bit as effectively as the mound with all of the bloated white roots wrapped around it.

It was only then that he noticed the thick matt of sticky webbing that clung to his boots; the spiders crawling all over the chamber had woven a web with him at its heart.

He tried to lift his boot, tearing the strands of the web, but more stretched than tore. There were too many spiders for him to make sense of climbing all over him, crawling up his legs, under the cuffs of his trousers, their legs itching like a rash as they found their way to his skin.

Faraday tried to shake them off, but the damned things wouldn't be budged.

The light from Gilroy's torch guttered alarmingly, the stench of burning meat suddenly filling the chamber as Gilroy Sinclair screamed. The flames had spread down his hand and wrist, carried by more spiders, the arachnids on a suicide mission. He dropped the firebrand, changing the entire layout of the chamber, banishing the shadows by their feet and scattering the crush of smaller spiders, only to turn everything from head height and above black.

Gilroy stamped and stamped at the ground, a mad man in a frantic dance as he tried to scuff out the flames before they ripped up his legs and engulfed him.

He couldn't pull his hand clear of the Spider God's abdomen. The silk of the web was like glue on his skin, sticking, sticking, sticking, no matter how frantically he pulled at it.

It was all Faraday could do to watch, but it was hard. A horror show. The flames ripped up him, his clothes searing and shrinking back on bubbling skin. And still he screamed, flailing around for help. Gilroy's hand grabbed at his, but Faraday shrugged it off and backed up a step, putting a little more distance between him and the burning man.

Behind Gilroy, the abdomen pulsed in time with the heat, faster and faster, the creatures within answering the flames.

The heat was incredible, but short lived. With nothing left to feed off, it burned out seconds after the initial rush of flame, leaving blistered and charred flesh along one side of Gilroy's body.

He was still alive.

Faraday saw the shimmer of tears reflected in his companion's eyes, but there was nothing he could do to help him. He couldn't drag the other man out of this place, then carry him through the forest. They didn't have the food or water between them. Not enough for two. It was a difficult choice, but in the end it was no choice at all. He backed away a step, and then another.

And then the sac started to rupture.

The shrieks that emerged from the Spider God were hideous. The chamber swelled with the chitinous cries of a million spiders being born to the world of fire, and dying in it almost as soon as they emerged from the birthing sac. They swarmed out, in numbers beyond counting, and still they kept coming. They scurried and skittered across the shadowy ground, over the bulbous roots, over Gilroy Sinclair, looking for ways *into* him. They were across his eyes, burrowing up his nose, into his ears. They crawled across his cracked lips and down into the wetness of his mouth, first one, then another, then more, until a constant stream of bloated ugly little spiders were swarming into his mouth and Faraday couldn't begin to imagine how more could cram themselves inside.

The rancid stench filled the chamber. Burned meat.

And up front, the mound shifted, something, the Spider God's head, emerged from where it had burrowed into the earth, shaking clear the clods of dirt. Pedipalps caked with mud, fangs dripping with poison, eyes shimmering with malicious intent. This was no dumb creature. There was a ferocious cunning behind those multifaceted eyes as it turned on him.

Faraday bolted into the darkness, desperately trying to reach the light. The twists and turns of the ramp filled with the insanity of millions of chittering voices, a constant teeming life, and frightened as he was, he couldn't find his way. He stumbled. He staggered. He lurched. He hit the wall. Hit another wall. The infernal chitter and skitter of tiny feet behind him in the darkness hounded him. He hit the wall again, and reached out, trying to feel his way along the cold stone, but the slickness wasn't lichen as he'd thought on the descent, it was spider silk, and it pulled at his hands, slowing his escape.

No townhouse in Bayswater was worth this.

He felt the slope of the ground beneath his feet begin to rise. On hands and knees, he crawled up, and up, feeling the first featherlight brush of spider's feet against his skin as he reached the next level, and more as he continued to crawl.

There should have been light by now.

But there was no light.

What was he thinking?

He had matches.

Faraday fumbled around in his khaki's for a spark, and dragged the match across the stone, even as he spilled more from the box, bringing enough light to the cramped passageway to see that where there should have been an arch, and columns, tangled vine and pitted stone, the passageway dead-ended. The damned natives had pushed a boulder across the entrance, trapping them in here with that thing!

He pushed at the stone. Clawed at it. Heaved. But no amount of pushing or clawing or heaving was going to budge it. It needed more brute strength than one man alone could manage.

"Ngumbo!" He howled at the rock. "Let me out, damn you! Let me out!"

He could scream himself sick, no one was coming.

Skitter. Scratch. Skitch. Skitter.

No, that wasn't strictly true.

Something was coming, just not someone.

Skitter. Scratch. Skitter.

Faraday pressed his back up against the stone as the match burned out between his fingers and plunged him back into darkness once more.

Skitter.

And still the arachnids crawled through the darkness towards him.

There was nowhere to hide.

No way out.

He was trapped in this hellhole. Death would either be fast, at the fangs of the Spider God, or slow, as his guts rotted and, with no food or water, he was forced to eat the only meat down here . . . Gilroy.

He screamed.

That only agitated the things down there with him.

They answered his screams with mocking high-pitched chitinous screams of their own, the Spider God's devoted subjects howling at the darkness. It was enough to drive a sane man out of his mind, and precious little of Malcolm Faraday remained sane as it was.

He slumped against the stone and waited for them.

They came, as he knew they would.

Faraday felt the skin-crawling first contact, like an itch he so desperately needed to scratch, but that was only the start of it. That tickle became so much worse as more and more of them found him. He felt them searching for a way inside, going for his ears and nose, trying to squeeze through his clenched teeth. Something inside his ear *popped*. He felt a trickle of wet sweetness followed by a cotton wool muffling of the world. They were in him. He opened his mouth to scream. That was a mistake. The damned things swarmed over his cemetery teeth, swelling to fill his throat, and even as he gagged and hacked and tried to cough more of them up, to purge his body, Faraday felt the searing sensation of a needlepoint piercing deep into the cerebral cortex of his brain, and with it came a flood of agonies as his body spasmed uncontrollably, legs kicking out, hands slapping, clenching, clawing, and his back arched away from the wall.

A single thought blossomed within his mind.

It was the voice of the Spider God.

Take me home.

He held out his hand, and a single spider crawled up onto his palm.

"I'm ready to leave this place," Faraday said with the voices of silks and wolfs, recluses, widows, bird-eaters and tarantulas, and all manner of arachnid down in this deep place, birthed by their god and queen, and now inside him.

The little spider scurried out through a chink too small for his eye to mark, in search of Ngumbo and the other Spider worshippers who had brought them face to face with their god. Seeing it emerge, they must have understood the significance, because a moment later stone ground against stone and a sliver of light appeared.

Faraday had no control of his body, as he stood and turned to face the light.

Slowly, that slice of light grew.

He emerged from the temple, feeling the light on his skin for the first time in millennia, and not owning any of his thoughts. Behind him, he heard a shuffle of movement. He did not need to turn to know that more of his children were in that charred body, lumbering to catch up. Where two had entered, thousands upon thousands emerged, carried in those bodies that would take them far away from this place, across the water to where those who had done so much harm to this place and her people—her, Faraday's mind was gone now, beyond any kinetic influence controlling the muscles and movement, his body was hers now and hers alone—where one by one she would dispatch her children to find the dark corners, the dank spaces, and from them, multiply, and at night, search out more soft flesh and weak minds to enter and control. She saw memories and faces, places like the Blackfriars Club and men of influence, and knew she had found the right host to make the Englishmen suffer for what they had done to her children and their homes.

"*Prim . . . it . . . ive cult . . .*," she heard Gilroy's brittle voice behind her, her spiders struggling to shape the words on their stolen tongue.

It brought a smile to her face.

"My queen," the man on his knees said, with all the passion of a fanatic. Ngumbo raised his head to look her in the eye. "How can we serve you?"

"I am hungry."

"There is meat," the man promised.

She shook her head. "No. Take me home."

ZOOPALOOZA

Guy Adams

HOLLYWOOD LOVES A cunt.

It's the only explanation for the bananas career of Manny Johns; that cloud of sweat and whisky fumes and straw, that festering, dangerous, weapon of a man. I mean . . . everybody knew who they were dealing with; this guy smeared his faecal heart on both sleeves of his tattered, plaid work jacket.

That jacket . . . forearms furred like seedpods, frayed like Jimmy Dean's soul. Chewed on by the best. That jacket will go on, crawling its way through the underbrush and dust of the canyons, hunting for coyotes to make howl. Haunted with spittle and piss and tears and blood.

Manny Johns and blood went together like pickle and burger. Scary motherfucker was born in blood and died the same way, screaming and wet.

But I'm getting ahead of myself.

The guy was legendary, that's all.

You ever find yourself cooing over the wet, sympathetic eyes of Dodie the Drifter? Course you did. Sap. That itchy-pawed mongrel who always sniffed out a sob-story and did his best to help? You were wet at the work of Manny Johns. He trained every damn one of those Dodies – and yeah, hate to piss on the magic, but a lot of hounds played that part, a pack of peripatetic pooches.

You ever wished you could ride on the back of Thunder? Clippity-clop pal to Danny Walker,

189

orphan and Gold Rusher across seven seasons of tv trash? It was Manny Johns that broke Thunder.

It was Manny Johns that broke them all.

Hollywood's most successful trainer and wrangler, the man that gave the silver screen every roar, every stampede, every winsome whinny worth a damn. If you loved an animal show at your local theatre, bet your last nickel you had Manny Johns to thank for it.

But I don't need to tell you that. You've heard stories about him, sure you have.

Did Manny Johns really kill a man for spitting on his tiger? Did he strip buck naked and ride Champion the Wonder Horse through the foyer of Grauman's? Did he piss in Ronnie Reagan's fruit punch and then demand, at gunpoint, that the "no-account little shit" slurp it up through a straw?

Did he really screw the biggest stars of 1954 on Frank Sinatra's tennis court, knees mottled by sod into rough-poured concrete? And if so, who did he fuck first, Ava Gardner or Lassie? And which made him cum-howl louder?

Stories in this town are bigger than the truth, but the truth of Manny Johns is simple: fucker was bad and he deserved what happened to him.

On the night it happened, the moon looked like something a sick dog would cough up. My back's killing me. The walk up Mulholland to get to Zoopalooza has near done me in – and I speak as someone who has skirted death a lot in her long, long life. By the time I'm stood under the bloodclot-red sign of the ranch, breathless, hot, ready to do damage, my mood is a couple of limes south of sour. I can actually hear the goddamned pain in my knees, burrowing bugs curling and crunching in the bones of me. Shitlickers.

I sit down in the long grass to find a little calm. Did the same back in my acting days. By God, I had a temper back then. I'd tear your goddamned face off at the least provocation . . . nearly cost me my career; hell, nearly cost me my life.

If it hadn't been for Johns.

The wind is being intrusive, ruffling my hair, giving me chills. For a minute I fear the old rage is going to come back. That rage don't plan. That rage don't watch its own back. That rage is the last thing I need.

After getting a few clear breaths, enough that I can hold myself steady – as steady as I manage, I'm old, something's always on the tilt – I get up and make my way past the sign and into the darkness.

I remember when this place first opened. All the press, all the hullabaloo. Johns called in favours and a press agent from MGM stepped up to tickle and tease. Tom Mix is there, only a few days away from checking out on the road to Phoenix. The ghost of movie westerns past, sweating beneath the brim of that twenty gallon hat. If any other famous faces were planned they're a no-show. This is early in the story of Manny Johns; give it a few years and you wouldn't be able to throw a pine cone around here without hitting someone beautiful in the eye.

Not that Johns ever needed anybody else to grab headlines for him. As the Zoopalooza sign was unveiled he appeared, oiled and loinclothed, riding on the back of Danny, his star lion. Danny reared up and roared as the cameras flashed and Johns, not inclined to let the cat get all the lines, gave a Tarzan roar that blew through the place like a factory siren.

Danny. Poor bastard. So beautiful, so noble on camera, so fragile off it. Always the way. Redhead wore a wig for the last few movies of his career, inclined, as he was, to tear out his own hair during long hours of misery in his cage.

I was there at his funeral, press pumped as the coffin was lowered into dry earth. Johns, head lowered, brim of his black safari hat pouring out a shadow that hid his bored, emotionless face as he dumped that lion in the dirt.

"King of the Jungle, ready to roar in Heaven" said the headstone, "loyal, loving and loved forever." Which was as sappy as the newspapers wanted. No mention was made that said loyal and loving lion met its maker along the blunted edge of Johns' wood axe. Johns wasn't one to abide waste, sure as hell wasn't going to expend a bullet on the old, twitching has-been.

Danny would have been sad to see me there, that night, working my way between cages, out of sight of the house. As much as he'd suffered, had cause to hate the bastard who had brought him to this, the tombstone truth stood, he always had been loyal.

My fingers don't move like they used to. There was a time when I could peel the skin off a dream, now it's all bent twigs and cracked knuckles. So it takes a time. The setting up. The wiring. The grunt work. It takes a time.

I'm feeling fizzy by the time things are on track. Shivers and shakes and excitement. When this pays off these old bones are going to feel things they ain't felt in years. I got neon crackle in my belly and it takes me back – as most things are of a mind to it seems – to the first time I set eyes on Johns.

I smelled him then saw him. Guess that's the way for most people. He had an odour to him that no bath or brush could handle. When Johns was upwind of you there was no doubting it. It was a rare day in the city that you would find yourself within nostril distance of a cow ranch making sweet, sweet fucks to an abattoir. Sprinkle a little sugar on top of that, a few handfuls to soak up the blood on the concrete floor, a kidney donut. Then a few splashes of bourbon, nothing expensive; even when the money was all but beyond counting, Johns never liked to sip anything that didn't burn. Wrap that up in leather and cyclamen toilet water – Johns splashed that stuff liberally, enough to make the Devil wrinkle his nose in Hell, claimed it made him feel 'fresh' – and you had the broader notes.

I was sitting in the shade of a fake palm tree on the MGM lot, wallowing in self-pity and anger and juggling wooden coconuts. Once again I'd blown my stack. Real big deal this time; I'd seen true red, grabbed myself one of the wooden swords the ersatz natives were waving about the place and promised all who'd listen that they could take as many inches of it as I could ram asswards. I screamed blood and thunder, I sure did. I wanted casualties. I wanted a mother-fucking death toll. Had to get out there lickity-split, real greased feet. That no-talent hack, Rollo Thorpe stooped to calling the studio cops, and I could see which way that would work out for me. I mean . . . I wasn't no Maureen O'Hara, you know? No second chances for me.

"What you doin', beautiful?" says Johns, in that tone he used before things turned shitsville.

Charming. That velvet-throated lie.

Now, I hadn't floated up the river a few weeks ago. I knew slippery charm when I heard it, but I was out of options. I could either make nice with the evil-smelling son of a bitch or I could smash out his brains with a wooden coconut. Both seemed fair in that moment – what I say about that rage, huh? Self-preservation kicked in and I decided to play pretty.

He sat down next to me and we danced around a while. You know. Give a little, take a little, never so much that you couldn't cut the other dead at any point. You learn that in Hollywood real quick; never give too much. We're all commodities out here and those bastards will spend you dry. In the end, not seeing much point in doing otherwise, I came clean on what had happened on set.

He leaned back and there was the yawn of stretching fabric, the medical brace I would later discover he always wore under his shirt. "Well," he said, "I figure a gal has a right to express herself once in a while." He scratched his face and his nails were filled with dirt; jetblack half-moons wedged deep beneath nicotine yellow claws. "I know well enough what people can be like on these cheap shows. All corners cut and to hell with anyone whose name isn't on the poster, am I right?"

Of course he was.

The studio cops turned up then, having finally tracked me down. I sighed, hung my head low and figured out that this useless career of mine had just about run its course.

"She's with me, boys," said Johns, getting up and holding out his hand to me. "And if you've got any problems you can write them up and post them right on to the complaints department of Zoopalooza Ranch. Or shove 'em up your ass, either way will get you the same response."

I took his hand and walked off the lot and into a new storm. It felt good for all of an afternoon, happiness until the sun set, ground out against the hills all bloody and orange. Then . . . Well, if it had worked out right you wouldn't find me out there in the dark, wiring up a way to fry that sick bastard would you? Huh? Would you? You wouldn't find me out there with that goddamn intrusive wind, and that smell of the stables, and the buzzing chiller motor of cicadas, and every single motherfucking thing just working on a way of killing that bastard, would you? Would you?!

No, you wouldn't.

It was time to rouse him from his bed and have some fun. Time for a little night orchestra. I played loud and proud across the bars of the cages, making tin plate and iron sing. The lions roared, the horses whinnied, the dogs barked, the birds screeched. It was a jungle out there in the darkness, and I almost felt calm as the sound of shock, surprise, terror and fear rose up into the late autumn sky and danced with the clouds.

Zoopalooza was a good few miles away from the closest neighbours; it had to be. This was not the first night to be filled with screaming. Life on Zoopalooza was lived loud. Training was given with spike and spark; it was a rare day without the smell of something alive cooking a little and expressing how goddamn much that hurt.

"In this life," Johns was heard to say, "nobody learns anything unless it hurts him. Lessons, the good ones, the ones that stick, are like tattoos, cut into you and there forever."

From the back of the ranch, I heard the door slam open; the click of a shotgun being loaded and the smell of Johns proceeded.

"What the hell is going on?" he shouted, as if the night air would set him straight, as if the key to solving all mysteries was just to roar skywards. I've spent more than enough time on my knees to know it don't get you far, not in the long run.

This was where my plans could have turned to shit and, you know what, if they had then I'd have taken both barrels and kissed this world goodbye. But I knew I had the advantage on Johns, always did, because he relied on muscles, never brains. Not saying he didn't have a good thought once or twice in his life, something just sharp enough you could have whittled a wooden whistle with it, but he didn't make a habit of it. Didn't think he had to.

So, I moved down the end of one of the big, empty cages – there were always empty cages, the residents of Zoopalooza didn't stay long – banging my knuckles against a steel feeding bowl, waiting for him to walk my way.

I watched the shadow of him, thinner than I'd last seen it, more hunched. Time even picks at Manny Johns it seemed.

The screaming around me was making things slippery. Hard to keep time on track. I've always had a weakness for it. The here and now, the then and when, get a little muddled at times. When you've taken the sort of beatings I have, lived this sort of life, you can't be surprised when things get loose. When things go fritz.

It was like everything that had been was *now*. Every whipcrack, every burst of electricity, every slap of stick on muscle, every crack of bone, every grunt, every roar, every scream, every promise, every last breath, every up and every down, and oh good god damn but it all gets so motherfucking slippery at times, yes it does, so slippery, oh jesus will you all just stand still?

"I know you?" Johns asks, and I get a grip on my thinking, get my eyes to focus, get my feet to feel the floor. I realise he's inside the cage and walking towards me.

"I know you?" he asks again. "You one of mine?"

And I want to answer. I want to press my ageing, dry, scarred face into his, and I want him to smell the rot on my breath, the blood and the stomach acid and the anger and Know Me. But, at the same time, I want to live long enough to hear that forgetful fucker die badly.

So I drop the water bowl and leap up, grabbing hold of the bars above. I hoist my legs and swing, hurling myself over him and towards the open gate of the cage. I move like an ape half my age; I move like an ape at the start of her career, when things might have gone better – but they wouldn't, of course they wouldn't, because it's no sensible monkey's business out here in the hills, and we all end up in shallow graves, no palmprint in the concrete for us.

I slam the gate shut and go to lock the padlock. Johns is on the move, no idiot; like all animals he knows when the predator is flexing their jaw. For a moment I think these old fingers are going to crash out on me; they freeze, arthritis flares and I think I'm going to get this far but no further. Which would suck at the movies but is pretty much how things go in real life most every day. Then, just as Johns comes crashing at me, trying to get the gate back open, the lock clicks shut and I fall back in the long grass and howl with happiness. I shake and roll, I punch the sky, I scream, I laugh, all while the rhythm section – Old Manny Johns and the iron gate – bang out their beat.

I'm fair exhausted by the time I get myself under control, but the fizz is in and the wind is high, and the smells are rich and the time is now.

"I do know you, don't I?" he says, peering through the bars.

I point at the scar that runs through my left eye. There's no guarantee he'll recognise it, even though he gave it to me only a few days after that first meeting at MGM, when he rescued me from Tarzan's Dumbest One Yet and a lethal injection. You didn't offer Weismuller a wooden assfuck and get away with your career or life. That puffy bastard never did have a sense of humour.

"I know you," he hisses. "Thought you were dead."

You and every fucking casting agent this side of the coast, I thought and held up the two keys to Johns future: the wired switch that would control the voltage through the floor of the cage he was in and the straight razor he could use when he'd had enough of it all.

I tossed the razor inside the cage and pressed the button for the first time.

UNCAGED

Paul Finch

IT WAS A three-day journey from Antioch to
Laodicea.

The caravan was larger than the average, one
of several reasons why two cohorts had been
drawn from the 6th to protect it. As always in this
scrubland, the soldiers marched two-by-two on
either side of the unpaved track, their heavy,
leather-clad shields turned outward, bronze
bosses glinting in the Syrian sun. But at no stage
did young Gaius feel in danger. These straight
roads and arid plains were vastly preferable to the
muddy paths and shadow-filled woods of the
Teutoberg. Admittedly, the climate here was
uncomfortable; scorching during the day, bitter at
night. But what had it been like on the Rhine?
When the rain wasn't pouring, the mist lay
blanket-thick. When winter came, snowflakes
flew like arrows on the northern wind.

But such was life on the frontiers of Empire,
and in some ways, as a seven-year-old finding his
way in the world, Gaius was proud of that. Not
that he wasn't glad to be returning to Antium.
The last time he'd been a babe-in-arms, so he
only had hazy recollections: rolling hills,
vineyards, warm sea-breezes. His mother would
be glad to be going home too, if she could only
shake herself out of mourning. She'd remained in
her chaise for the whole trip thus far, draped in
widow's weeds, clutching his father's urn.

Gaius was sad about his father too. But
constant hard soldiering had been no easy

bedrock on which a man could build a relationship with his infant son. It seemed to Gaius that he'd only ever resided in military camps, safe behind the ramparts and ballistae, but rarely seeing his father. In truth, he'd rarely seen much of anything. That was one reason he was enjoying this journey, the world unfolding as he processed grandly through it.

And then, of course, there were the animals.

The caravan was crammed with the usual exotic traders, one of whom, a hoary old Greek called Xeno, had over a dozen cages containing a variety of beasts, which he intended to sell to the marshals of the arena in Rome. It wasn't that Gaius was especially childish where animals were concerned; he knew this particular batch was bound for vicious slaughter, but he still found them fascinating. In this group alone there were several breeds he'd never seen before. The sleek, tawny lions were familiar enough, as were the leopards, the hyenas, the lynx. But there were others Gaius had only heard about, and some that he'd presumed were myth.

Despite sapping midday heat, he rode back along the caravan on his gelding. Xeno, a corpulent, sun-wizened oldster, always wrapped in Bedouin garb and nestled under a silken parasol, cantered up to meet him. Gaius and the old beast-master had become friends since they'd set out from Antioch. If the lad's status as the scion of Roman patricians had a part to play, he was unconcerned. A friend was a friend.

"You help me feed my pets?" Xeno asked.

"You're feeding them?" Gaius said. "That's wonderful."

Xeno turned his horse around. "Come with me, come."

Like many merchants in these parts, the Greek spoke a range of languages, most of them so second-nature to him now that he often mingled them in a curious dirge, which only his sons and slaves appeared to find comprehensible. It was ironic that his command of Latin was a lesser power, though he had enough of it for Gaius to understand something of the knowledgeable, rambling lectures he gave on the varied wildlife he traded in.

The animals were enclosed in the caravan's centre, in wheeled cages with dusty awnings thrown over them when the sun was high. Xeno was always happy to lift these awnings and let the lad peek in. At present, as promised, they were feeding, so the drapes were thrown aside and food – joints of beef for the carnivores, foliage for the rest – was lowered through open hatches in the cage roofs, the only means of ingress while the caravan was in motion. Each cage had a barred gate, though these were securely locked and Xeno held the keys personally.

After watching the lions and leopards eat, they rode on to the section where the rarer specimens could be found: a ponderous hippo still caked in a crust of river-slurry; a rhinoceros with a curved sabre of bone on its nose; and perhaps most spectacular of all, a monstrous crocodile, which lounged under a heap of rank straw, but at twenty feet in length was never able to conceal itself completely. Gaius marveled at its great leathery bulk, at its thick, overlapping scales, at the narrow eyes fixed unblinkingly on him over its bony dragon-snout.

"If he's a water animal, Xeno . . . can he endure this heat?"

The Greek nodded, impressed by the sensible question.

"This crocodile – he endure anything. I water him, yes. But I find this beast in the market of Caesarea. Before that, he come from Nile Valley in Egypt, through desert so hot, so burned that this place is nothing." Xeno jabbed a fat, beringed finger at the hunks of dried meat scattered amid the dung and sawdust of the cage floor. "He sooner eat us living, no, than any of this – how you say, rubbish? This shit."

They moved onto the giraffe, which was so tall that its head protruded through the topmost bars of the cage, and the slaves had to feed it by thrusting up wads of hay on the ends of spears. Finally, at the rear, they came to the beast that, as far as Gaius was concerned, was the strangest in the collection.

Again, it was feeding. On top of the cage, a slave mopped sweat from his brow, and lowered a bucket of swill on a rope. At first, the beast in the cage paid it no mind. Instead, it glared steadily at its audience, its eyes moist, deep-set and brown. In essence it was a common enough creature. A wild hog of the sturdy, coarse-haired sort found in the wilderness all across the Empire, but its feral appearance would churn the guts of any gladiator having to face it. It was a boar, but even on that basis was huge, twelve hands at the shoulder, with a great, ridged hump. That alone would make it a formidable opponent, but there was more to it yet. Its breadth was awesome, ox-like, and it stood balanced on solid haunches of muscle. Its neck was so thick that its head seemed to sprout from its torso, though that head was huge and flat, an anvil of bone covered in black, matted hair. Its mass of tusks curled and twisted in fantastical shapes.

It was all the more mysterious thanks to the story surrounding its capture. Gaius had been told that it put up so ferocious a fight when they'd snared it that several men died. It had resisted nets, spears, even drug-smeared arrowheads. Allegedly, they'd discovered it in a place of ancient tombs, where rumours about an evil force had kept local folk at bay. The lad eyed the animal nervously as it consented to eat the swill, grunting and snuffling, great slops falling to either side of the bucket.

"Xeno, tell me again about that place where you caught him."

"Ah!" Xeno nodded. "Gadarene. East of the Galilee Sea." He shook his head. "A bleak place, yes. Empty. And always the wind you hear, howling. Always howling like these spirits of the dead. A people live there, they call the Gergasenes." He indicated the boar. "A wild folk, but this . . . *thing*, and others like it, they lay waste this region. Terrorising these people."

"That's no way for pigs to behave."

Xeno clapped his hands, signalling a slave to bring him a goblet of watered wine. When he'd slaked his thirst, he continued. "They say it fault of a rabbi. He come first and cast out devils from madman who live there. In those tombs . . ." He shook his head. "This madman, he kill all travellers. He beat, rob, kill. Then the rabbi come, and he cast out these devils. And the madman . . . is himself again. Is cured. But the devils, they go into these swine. These swine here."

The boar had resumed watching them in sullen, eerie silence. Xeno slapped his fleshy thigh. "Is ghost story, no? Should be good for price when I sell in market at Rome."

"What happened to the others?" Gaius asked. "The other pigs, I mean. Didn't you say there were more?"

"Many more. First, they run, then they stand and fight, then they run. The ones we no catch, they go straight into sea. They drown. This one here – he claim four men. He gore them so bad they die, he trample their bodies, he toss them, bite them."

"He doesn't look like any wild pig I've ever seen," Gaius said.

"Is why I say to them: 'Hey, you put him with finest gladiator in circus.' Even then, I put wager on this beast here."

When the attack came, it was unexpected. Though in truth it should not have been.

Tiberius Caesar had been on the imperial throne five years and was proving an efficient and dutiful heir to the great Augustus. The coffers of the Empire brimmed, her armies stood at maximum strength, her administration resided in the hands of incorruptible men. Contentment reigned, even here in the east, where Syria rubbed shoulders with the lands of the Parthians and their king, Artabanus. But this was the least settled of all the Roman provinces. Artabanus had long had difficulty controlling his warlike nobility – or *cataphracti,* as the Greeks called them – and though he, himself, was wily enough to avoid direct conflict with his powerful neighbour, his excitable subjects held it an ancestral right to raid whenever it suited them.

"*Parthians! Parthians!*"

Gaius turned in his saddle. There was a squealing and creaking as reins snapped and brakes bit and, one by one, the vehicles came to a standstill. The legionaries on either side of the road halted too, turning outward to face the plain. At the barked commands of officers, they unslung packs and hefted javelins over the tops of shields. From a nearby ridge, the lad now saw a great press of horsemen, maybe three or four-hundred, hurtling downhill in a swirl of dust. Behind them, sunlight glinting on their coats of articulated iron plate, the *cataphracti* lurked. These too were mounted, but armed with lances whereas their common men carried bows made from horn and tensioned wood.

The legionaries held their ground, but there were panicked shouts from the merchants and their retainers. All jocularity gone, Xeno roared out orders to his people, urging his mount forward, drawing a blade from a scabbard by his saddle. His sons wheeled their horses about until they came alongside him, while his mercenary troop formed a protective line in front of the cages. These latter were Thracians, Numidians and Scythians. Brute races, as their leather corselets and dusty, dented helmets attested, but skilled in war. Each man carried his weapon of choice, from the curved *falcata* to the long, straight-edged *spatha*.

This was a carefully rehearsed deployment, but things were happening at bewildering speed. Before Gaius knew it, there was a whistle of incoming arrows. Someone screamed, and he spotted a Nubian slave drop his spear and stagger, a feathered shaft transfixing his naked thigh, dark arterial blood jetting copiously. Not unduly alarmed, for he had seen this before, Gaius stood in his stirrups and peered along the caravan, trying to make out the action further afield.

The legionaries had now formed rigid lines, the merchants and their people clustering around the goods and wagons, brandishing any weapons they could. The oncoming horde approached from the east, but the troops who'd been stationed westward held their positions, backs firmly turned to the attackers. This was as it should be; it was a common Parthian strategy to strike from both sides at once, but only to launch the second assault several minutes after the first so that half the defenders would have been drawn out of position.

There was a hiss and a metallic clatter.

Gaius half-ducked, but it was only luck that saved him, for an arrow had struck the bars of the nearest cage and ricocheted away. Realising his position was perilous, he leaped from the saddle, tethered his gelding, and clambered up the ladder to the top of the cage. Here, some ten feet up, he could stay low but keep good vantage on the battle.

But this was not the kind of fighting that Roman troops liked.

The Parthians refused to engage. Up close, despite the clouds of dust erupting from their horses' hooves, he could see them more clearly; their colourfully-embroidered shirts and caps, their baggy trousers and hook-toed boots, their bearded, nut-brown faces. They never ventured closer than thirty or forty yards from the first line of legionaries, but galloped back and forth, loosing arrows at a mesmerising rate. The legendary 'Parthian shot', which Gaius had heard so much about, was on constant display. With uncanny skill, a bowman would approach at a furious charge, rein sharply, skid-turn and shoot an arrow behind him, moments later circling around to do the same again, and again. Their missiles were light, of course, and though driven by the powerful double-curved bows, tended to skate off the legionaries' body-plate, though this wasn't always the case.

Like many in the east, the men of the 6th Legion tended to customise their equipment to suit the harsh environment. This included sensible adaptations like the attachment of a cloth at the back of the helmet to protect the neck from the glare of the sun, or the removal of greaves and heavy leggings. Unfortunately, it also involved discarding the mail-coat traditionally worn beneath the plate. Most legionaries did this to reduce their weight for the long march, but under a Parthian arrow-storm it became a distinct disadvantage. Occasionally, an arrow would hit a soldier's plating at such angle that it would punch through. Alternately, it might find a chink between plates and penetrate with even greater force. Even as Gaius watched, several legionaries went down, wounded rather than killed, though one – by the transverse crest on his helm, a centurion – had been pierced through the right eye, and was dead before he hit the ground.

The Parthians' overall plan would be difficult to gauge. They knew that a continued assault of this nature would finally prove intolerable to the Romans, and that units of cavalry would be sent back from the vanguard to engage them. It might then become a running fight, or perhaps the raiders would withdraw. But there were other possible outcomes. The purpose of the attack was to purloin the baggage, which was why, though diversionary assaults were being made up and down the caravan, the bulk of the enemy were focussed *here*. It might therefore be that the tribune would decide discretion was the better part of valour, and order the baggage-train cut loose. This would outrage the merchants, but alone they knew they'd be overwhelmed and slaughtered, and so ultimately they would leave with the legionaries.

Whichever, the arrow-showers would continue for some time yet.

Gaius lay flat on the planking atop the cage, watching.

More Parthians appeared, this time on the western horizon. There were several hundred, and they came at a fast gallop. Seconds later the sky was dark with their arrows, the feathered missiles sleeting down among the legionaries, clanking as they bounced off plate, or thudding as they embedded in the leather and plywood of the soldiers' shields. Civilians were picked off more easily. For the most part, these were the traders' slaves. They were among the least well-armoured, and yet were expected to stand to the fore and be brave. They fell one after another, but they weren't the only ones. Some of the merchants themselves were struck from their saddles. One of Xeno's sons, Siciles, was hit in the throat, dropping backward over his horse's tail. Xeno cursed, but he had lost sons before and had many left yet, so no tears appeared on his seamed, sun-burnished cheeks.

The Parthians also suffered. The legionaries launched javelins, and though these were speculative shots, one or two found their mark. A Parthian horse was wounded in the flank, and with frenzied screams commenced a furious bucking and kicking, depositing its rider in the dirt. He scrambled to his feet, only for a second *pilum* to strike him between the shoulders. On the western flank, believing the previous attack would have drawn off most of the defence, the raiders came closer, straying into range not just of the Romans' *pila*, but of the slings and bows of the private soldiers. A few were knocked from their saddles, some so close to the line that defenders broke out and butchered them where they lay. Gaius saw one Parthian dragged shrieking and struggling into the midst of the caravan, where what seemed like a hundred blades left him a ripped-open carcass barely reminiscent of humanity.

So engrossed was the lad that he scarcely noticed how close the combat had come to his own position. When he realised that furious blows were being exchanged directly below him, it was too late to get away. He crawled to the edge of the cage roof and gazed down, bemused that the Parthians had joined at close quarter – and saw the reason why.

The *cataphracti* had arrived. Three of them had galloped down from the eastern ridge, and with lances levelled, had charged clean through the first line of legionaries, sending men tumbling like skittles, skewering others like chickens on spits. Now with swords drawn, they rode in and out of Xeno's band, cutting and thrusting.

Gaius had been around soldiers all his life, and had seen at first-hand the many enemies of Rome, but he was awed by the magnificence of the *cataphracti* up close. Their polished coats of scale covered their bodies from wrist to throat, and hung to their ankles in long, clinking skirts. They wore iron gauntlets and tall, plumed helms, and their swords – straighter and longer even than the Celtic *spatha* – rose and fell like cleavers in an abattoir. Blood sliced the air as skulls were

209

sundered, limbs lopped. There were frantic, guttural shouts, cries more terrible than Gaius had ever heard. For the first time, it occurred to him that he himself might be killed or, even worse, captured.

In the wake of their leaders, the Parthian horse-archers drove in closer, unleashing their shafts at pointblank range. This was their last push, Gaius realised; their final, desperate attempt to wrest something from the caravan. They were throwing in everything they had, and the line of legionaries had broken under the pressure.

Then, in a single second, the tide turned.

A *cataphract* slumped sideways, felled by a blow from a mattock wielded by Xeno himself. The weight of the heavily-armoured horseman overbalanced his mount; it staggered, squealing, and blundered against the cage, the entire frame of which shook. There was violent movement from the straw-filled space inside, and Gaius rose to his feet, alarmed. Scenting the blood of the Parthian leadership, several legionaries abandoned their rigid ranks and joined the melee, swords flailing. The remaining *cataphracti* turned their steeds about and tried to hack their way to freedom, leaving Xeno and his men to slash and stab at their wounded comrade. Rent from all sides, streaked with its own blood and that of its master, the animal reared up and kicked hard, slamming its hooves into the bars of the cage. Again, the vehicle rocked. Gaius tottered away from the edge, for an arrow to flash by with inches to spare. In natural reflex, he wafted at it, stepping further backward . . . into nothingness.

He dropped, the iron frame of the hatchway cracking against the back of his skull, knocking him senseless as he twisted down through dusty air, landing heavily on another layer of planks, these softened by a great matting of rank straw.

At first, Gaius was unsure where he was.

Only slowly did he come to sense that he wasn't alone.

With a stench of ordure, something huge came clumping towards him. He glanced up from where he lay, though his vision was weak and watery, and all he could make out was a gross, misshapen object: an object with pin-point flames for eyes, an object that slavered hot drool through its lattice-work of ivory tusks.

A unique kind of fear gripped the lad.

The sounds of the battle raging beyond the bars faded.

Yet there was no attack; no goring; no tossing; no biting. Instead, the thing lowered its brutish slab of a head until its flattened snout was almost in contact with Gaius's face. The fat, pink nostrils quivered, dabbled with mucus. Unimaginably foul air gushed out, half-suffocating him. From somewhere inside the beast came a low, continuous rumble that was either a snarl rising from rancid guts, or a gentle purr.

Paralysed with fear, Gaius snapped his eyes shut. It breathed on him again, almost choking him. Such was the foulness in that breath that it was impossible to imagine it had come from any animal that was still alive.

But alive it was. As the lad lay curled in its humped shadow, it breathed upon him a third time, and a fourth, and a fifth. Each breath hung in a noxious cloud, filling his nose and throat, searing the soft tissues of his lungs. And suddenly, from some distant yet fast-approaching place he heard the squeals and grunts of its mad, dying kin. Horrible images swept over him: a haze of molten heat and through it a river of marauding swine spilling downhill into a tumult of mud and brine. Dozens of bodies floated there – whether human or hog he couldn't quite tell – pallid, hairless, bloated, many gruesomely bitten and torn. A crimson tide sloshed around them, thick and pungent as sewage.

So real was the heat and stink of it that Gaius tried to scream. But couldn't.

He couldn't make any sound at all – just a mindless grunting and snorting.

It was only as the tail-end of the Parthian war party rode away that Xeno turned and spotted Gaius lying huddled inside the cage of the Gadarene boar.

For all that he'd just been fighting for his life and his livelihood, the Greek was especially horrified by this. With wild cries, he summoned what remained of his band, dismounted and hurried to the bars. By the hatchway hanging open in the roof, it was easy to see what had happened, but it was difficult, if not impossible, to tell to what extent the youth had been injured. The boar lay at the opposite end of the cage. Possibly it had been hit by a stray arrow, though Xeno was scarcely worried about that.

All that mattered was the boy. How savagely would the beast have mauled him? Had it slain him? Gaius's mother would have their skins.

With spears and nets, two of Xeno's sons let themselves into the cage. The rest of the band, most still breathless and soaked with sweat, some clutching wounds, watched through the bars. They had all seen this brute on the rampage, and knew its ferocity. Though it *did* appear to be dead; in fact, on second glance, it *was* dead, for it already appeared shrunken and hollow under its desiccated hide. They eyed it warily as they reached in and tried to grab hold of the lad.

It was a great relief when, before they even got to him, he glanced up and started crawling shakily towards them.

"Good, good, you come now," Xeno quietly urged.

Once emerged from the cage, Gaius was ashen-faced but undamaged. He looked at the beast-master, though there was little recognition in his glassy eyes. Xeno's sons shut the gate and padlocked it. Still, the boar lay in its far corner, a moldering heap of flyblown fur and protruding bones.

The lad stumbled as he walked around. His eyes roved the aftermath of the battle. The Parthians, in their final rush to take the caravan, had paid a high price. Perhaps a hundred of their corpses strewed the vicinity. A few twitched feebly, still alive. The Romans stalked among them, occasionally stopping to deal a fatal blow with spear or *gladius*. Of Xeno's party, his dead son was being carried away. Several of his slaves had also died, but lay where they had fallen. The rest gathered arrows and stones, or patched gashes on the sweat-foamed flanks of their horses. Overhead, vultures already flew in crisscrossing patterns.

A loud laugh from Xeno interrupted the lad's thoughts. The Greek clapped his shoulders and gripped him by the face, a big, hot hand cupping either check.

"You live, eh? You live. Is good."

"I live," Gaius confirmed.

"Is good, yes, indeed."

"I must find mother."

"Ah!" Xeno nodded vigorously. "She's safe. Legion guard on pain of decimation."

Gaius didn't answer. He drifted away along the caravan, walking slowly, occasionally tottering, though gradually he straightened himself up. The Greek stared after him. The lad might be dazed, but he was polite and kind by nature, which was unusual for his breeding. As such, it was a mite worrying that he refused to exchange greetings with the surviving legionaries, or ask after those who had fallen. This was especially odd given that he had always been popular with the troops. When he was very young, they'd awarded him an army nickname. The rank and file still referred to him by it: 'Bootikin'.

It sounded a little childish, Xeno supposed, especially for a lad who was growing up. But Gaius seemed to like it, so where was the harm? And in any case, it didn't sound too ridiculous in Latin: Ligu-something or other. No, that was it . . . *Caligula*.

IN THE COURT
OF THE CRIMSON COW

Emma Riddell

SCOTT PULLED ON his walking boots, making sure the laces were taut before he tied them. The last thing he wanted was for them to come undone, stepped on, making him trip and end up with him falling down a cliff face. He put on his breathable waterproof jacket, grey hat with the obscene orange bobble, went through to the kitchen, filled up his water bottle, grabbed a packet of Squares and a Mars Bar. He paused. Then grabbed a second Mars bar. Just to be safe.

He kissed his wife Tabitha on the way out and ruffled his elderly dog's head, sad that the long walks that they used to go on were no longer. Godzilla was riddled with arthritis and it wasn't going to be long before he would have to be put down. The drugs that he was on were expensive, but every moment bought delayed the inevitable for that little bit longer.

Scott took the keys from the hanger by the door and saying "see you later!" was off.

The car was parked at the bottom of the hill; next door had bought a new car and it was parked in Scott's usual place, much to his chagrin. He made a mental note to get in touch with the council to apply for a dropped kerb. It would cost a few grand to get it sorted and for the front of his garden to be concreted over, but Scott liked throwing money at problems and he'd do anything to get one over on Frank, his weird and elderly neighbour who loved to show off his emaciated body while doing the mowing. As he was doing right that moment.

"Allright Scott, you want to borrow some of my CDs? You've never answered any of my Facebook messages." Frank asked, scratching the grey chest hair with his dirty fingers. It made Scott want to hurl.

"No, I don't. Fuck off and leave me alone," he said, without thinking. Frank was visibly shocked.

"No need for language like that, you miserable prick," he said, and fired the mower back up to drown out any reply Scott might make.

"Bloody hell, what was I thinking?" Scott said to himself as he got into the car, but his smile was the biggest it had been for months. It was stupid, but satisfying.

Scott drove through the city, only cursing at one driver who cut in front of him, "why can't you drive normally like every other cunt!" and twenty minutes later was driving into deep country.

His first stop was at Inchbrook golf course. At this time of the morning there would be one or two people who would be playing, but the last few holes, the sixteenth to the eighteenth, would be empty and Scott would be able to go about his business in peace.

He parked his car at the side of the road, jumped over the gate and walked parallel to one of the holes then cut across it diagonally. He arrived at the seventeenth a minute later and walked straight to the green.

It was covered in mushrooms.

"Yes!" he uttered, pulled a bag out from his jacket and started to gather the liberty caps. He counted as he picked and was happy that he had managed to get thirty decent mushrooms.

He made his way to the eighteenth hole and there again, the treasure that he was seeking. There were even more mushrooms here and he picked fifty.

Scott made his way back to the car quickly, and once he was in it, put the bag of magic mushrooms in the glove compartment.

He started the car and was off, driving to his next destination.

If you had asked Scott why he, at thirty-nine years of age, had decided that it was time to dabble with magic mushrooms, seventeen since he had last sampled any, he would have told you the truth. He was simply bored. He was happy at home, he loved Tabitha and Godzilla but if the lockdown had taught him anything, there was only so much television you could watch before you went mental. He had thought long and hard about asking Tabitha if she wanted to be involved—they had met at Marley House, both grinding their teeth, when they were eighteen and had been together ever since. Then came the bad trip one awful January night on her twentieth birthday and Tabitha ended up in hospital. It was then they decided never to do drugs again.

Scott was hesitant in bringing the subject up and when he did she was keen, but she said that she would have preferred some ecstasy; however the chances of them knowing anyone who could point them in the direction of a dealer were almost non-existent. They didn't live in that world any more and the one dealer they had known topped himself ten years ago.

So Scott had researched the best places outside of Bludborough to find magic mushrooms, and the forums said that the best places were either golf courses, where the greens were constantly maintained, or out in the open countryside, preferably where cows grazed and shat. The place he was heading to now, the forums suggested, had the best year on year crops. So Mortstone on the A978 was his final destination. A nice morning ahead, walking the fields, staying away from any cows, but taking great delight in examining their pats and seeing what was growing out of them. Scott thought that it was amazing that the seeds and spores that a cow ate while grazing didn't get broken down by acid, travelled through their four stomachs and were passed out safely and ready to grow.

Scott pulled into the layby, turned off the engine and saw the green fields that led into a forest. On the other side of the forest was moorland that stretched out for miles. He got out of the car, made sure that it was locked, and put his keys in the small rucksack that had his provisions, a small pen knife and an emergency space blanket made out of thin foil. Just in case. He put the rucksack on and he was off, climbing over the first barbed wire fence that took him into the field.

He made good time through the fields and the forest wasn't too thick; Scott only once having to force his way through the unwieldy branches like a bumblebee trying to style its way out of a spider's web. Out the other side of the forest the land was grass, partial bog, heather and large stones jutting out from the ground, like moss-covered teeth. Scott smiled, took a deep breath in and started to search the ground. He scored instantly, or at least he thought he did. The mushrooms, five in all, were growing out of the earth. They were a dark brown and had the tell-tale nipple on top with almost black gills underneath. Certainly not a liberty cap, the gills were too dark to be *Psilocybe fimetaria*...they *looked* like *Panaeolus olivaceous,* a type that mainly grew in the US and Canada, but there had been reports of it growing in the UK. Scott was rewarded when he opened his plant identifier app. Yes! They were *Panaeolus olivaceous* – do **not** ingest, they are poisonous – yadda yadda. He picked four of them and put them in the bag. The fifth one was a little mushy, so he squelched it between his fingers, looking with fascination at the black ink that spilled over his fingertips. Then he realised with horror what he had done, wiped his fingers on his jeans, got the bottle of water from his backpack and tried to wash the black stain off. It wouldn't budge.

Fuck. *Fuck.* Had he, by osmosis, taken the psilocybin in through his skin? Was he going to be tripping his bollocks off in an hour or so? He shook his head as he imagined the compounds fixing to blood cells and racing through his body, where the drug would latch onto neuroreceptors in his brain and the fun would begin.

"I have to get home, I have to get home, just in case," he said to himself. He put the meagre offerings into his backpack and took a swig of water. His mouth had suddenly gone dry. He knew what it was. The fear. The paranoia that he had fucked up, that something was about to go south because he didn't think. That he would come up whilst driving home and think an oncoming lorry looked like a marshmallow that he would want to crash into it and start eating.

He rang Tabitha. She picked up on the third ring. He told her what he had done.

"I think you're overreacting," his wife said calmly. "One mushroom, what's it going to do to you even if it could seep through that tough skin of yours? Make you go a little fuzzy around the edges? You'll be fine. Just get in the car and come home. I'll have a nice glass of orange juice ready for you; the Vitamin C will help get rid of any nasty enzymes you've got left in you."

She paused, letting the old myth about the juice do its job. She knew it was bollocks, she was hoping her husband didn't know, or had forgotten.

"Shit, you're right! I forgot about orange juice!" Scott said, and his voice sounded relieved. "I'm going to drive to the nearest garage and down a litre of Orangina."

It was then he heard the noise coming off from his right. A low moan. As if from someone, or something, in pain. Scott knew that it was impossible for anything to kick in that fast. He decided that whatever the noise was, it was real, and that he should go and see where it was coming from, just in case it was a walker who had broken their leg and fallen down behind a rock or something. He made his way cautiously. Climbing up a small hill, the sun broke free from the clouds and, not for the first time, Scott was taken aback by how beautiful his surroundings were; he and his missus should really take more stock of what was on their doorstep instead of staying in and binging Netflix box sets. Yes, *Squid Game* was fun, but did it have any wider meaning than to satisfy an itch once you got past the first episode?

The noise came again. It certainly wasn't human, but it sounded like it was in pain. He walked quickly now, and at the back of a large rock that had swirls and other shapes carved into it – no doubt something that his ancestors had worshipped at a millenia or more ago – there it was, a calf, god knows how old, but on its back, it's eyes large with panic, its nostrils flaring.

"Oh shit, where's your mum?" Scott said, looking round for its parents. They were nowhere to be found.

It was then he saw the awful hole on its thigh, huge, bloody and full of squirming maggots. Scott nearly threw up. To think that the poor thing had been walking around while flies laid eggs in the hole, that it had slowly got worse and worse, and then the eggs hatched. It was astounding that it hadn't yet been finished off by magpies or rooks.

The calf moaned, ending in a ragged gasp as it tried to get up again, but it was simply too weak. Scott pulled out his phone and tried to contact a vet, but there was no reception. He looked up at the stone the calf was sheltering against.

There was a large sharp shard of rock, a metre and a half in length, that was balancing on top of the rock the cow was lying against. How many thousands of years had it been on top of that one? Scott knew that it would be easy enough for him to climb up on top of it, but the thought of trying to push the slab onto the cow was truly horrifying. Scott didn't know if he had it in him. But he couldn't let the calf suffer; walking away and leaving it to die an agonizing, lonely death would be so much worse. Best to have a quick and painless death. That made up Scot's mind. He scrambled up onto the rock and pushed down hard on the shard. It wobbled. He knelt down and grabbed the underside of the shard and, with sweat instantly breaking out all over his body with the effort, pushed and moved, pushed and moved. After a while he slowly managed to inch it forward, waiting for that moment when gravity would take control.

With a loud *kkkkcrrrchhh* the slab slowly slid off. The sharp point of it cleaved through the calf's head and went deep into the soft earth. It couldn't have gone any better. Scott peered over, disgusted at his handiwork. He threw up. Once he finished heaving he slid off the rock himself, landing solidly on both feet. If anyone came across it, they would simply think it was an unfortunate accident. He breathed heavily, the exertion making his lungs hurt. He placed his hand against the ancient rock. It was warm to touch and he pulled his hand back sharply. The ancient carvings in the stone appeared to be luminescent, glowing in the gloam.

It was then he heard a mass of high-pitched bellows. Scott looked up; there was a herd of cows, around fifteen or twenty in total, high up on the hill, looking at him. He stepped back away from the dead calf, holding his hands up.

"I was just putting it out of its misery!" he shouted up at them. One of the cows stepped forward. It made a loud lowing noise, as if it was a command. The other cows stepped forward in unison.

"No way. This isn't normal cow behaviour," Scott thought, his mind racing. But Scott wasn't stupid. He turned and bolted towards the woods.

His headstart was a good one, but the cows thundered down the steep incline regardless. Several of them fell hard and tumbled over as they tried to keep up with the lead cow, snapping their legs and slamming into the earth.

Scott fled through the woods, unmindful of the pain caused by branches that whipped and caught him as he made his way through them to the fields. His chest was heavy and tight, unused to the sudden burst of energy that he demanded from his body. He no longer heard the thunderous noise that the cows were making, and then he was out of the other side of the woods. He veered off to his left so he could get a viewpoint of where he had been. The cows had been felled, lying in heaps in several places, all severely injured, bar one. It was a large female, and it stood at the bottom of the hill. It made a deep mooing noise, loud and terrifying.

"You're all fucking mental! All I did was try and help, and look at what you've done to yourselves!" he screamed, but the wind whipped away his voice. He turned and ran across the fields, back to the car.

He drove off towards home, the cow staring at him until he disappeared.

He did not come up by osmosis and did not tell his wife of his experience.

As it was a slow news week, the story was a big one. The farmer, being interviewed by the local station, was at a loss as to how the calamity happened, but he made his point by saying that he'd lost thousands of pounds worth of livestock, and having to put down so many injured animals was one of the hardest things he had ever had to do.

"I just can't understand or explain it. Something spooked them. Someone spooked them. Only one survivor, but try as we might we can't contain her. She's evading us at every turn, so I suppose we've lost her as well, unless I get lucky. The truth will out at some point, I suppose."

Scott felt awful. He half-expected the police to turn up at his door and ask him about his involvement, but nobody ever did.

When Scott finally got round to having the mushrooms a few months after the incident, dried covertly in the airing cupboard, a place his wife never went into, he had an *amazing* time on them.

Twelve Years Later

"Jesus, this is some walk you're taking us on," Scott puffed, removing his jacket and tying it round his ample waist. Dave turned around and grinned, his face glowing with effort. "This stuff gives you life man! And it's not as if you couldn't do with the exercise . . ." He left the statement hanging in the air between them and Scott knew it was true. Ever since the divorce he had spent his time working at the computer and eating for comfort. The trips to the gym became less frequent, before they stopped altogether.

It was a cold day, the clouds chasing the sun across the sky, the heather underfoot springy. Dave started to walk quicker and Scott shouted at him to go ahead, that he'd catch up.

His phone pinged. He looked at it. Tabitha. His heart sank.

Can you pick Shannon up from school?

He replied:

Sorry, no can do. Am up the hills with Dave. Doing a spot of walking. You'll have to find an alternative.

Tabitha was quick to answer.

Scott, you *have* to come back and pick her up. I'm not taking no for an answer. The babysitter cancelled and Richard is taking me to the theatre.

Richard. The prick Tabitha left him for.

Then that's a *hard* no. Enjoy your night watching the telly.

No answer for a couple of minutes. Then:

You cruel bastard. I could go for full custody you know. I'm sure the family courts would love to hear about all of your acid trips and that drug dealer you allowed to crash out at our house for two weeks while he was hiding from people he owed money to! Jesus! Just pick her up!

Scott smiled.

Yes, I'm sure they would frown. I'm too far away, I'd never get back in time. And remember, Tabitha, I've never told the court about your—

Scott's foot found air, no ground, and he went over, hard, and tumbled down a steep hill. His phone went flying, his boot was wrenched off his left foot and he heard a loud crack as a bolt of pain tore up that leg. He rolled and rolled down the hill, hitting jutting rocks and tussocks. A few ribs went, probably his wrist.
Then he slammed into a rock.
Lights out.

When Scott came to, he saw a cow looking at him. It had a silver-grey face, big eyelashes.

"Go get help," he joked, and that was when the pain really hit him. He screamed. The cow took several steps back, alarmed by the noise he was making. Scott tried to push himself up, and his good hand slipped on something. He tried again, and realised what it was, a greasy mould-green bone. He threw it away from him, and slowly sat up against the stone. It was then he saw the other slab of stone that was next to him, jutting out of the ground.

He twisted around and looked at the time-worn images that had been carved into the rock he was sitting against. The carvings seemed to be pulsing with a sickly-green light.

The calf. Memories came flooding back.

"Oh fuck," he shrilled, his voice breaking with panic. "Are you . . . you . . . I'm not a bad man, I just put it out of its misery is all."

The cow opened her mouth and a deep low came out. It nuzzled and rubbed against Scott's head. When it retreated, Scott saw that his blood had completely covered the cow's silver face. With one last look at him, she walked away from Scott and around to the back of the slab of rock that he had managed to push off all of those years ago.

The ungulate kicked the slab with her back leg. There was a large cracking noise and the stone moved an inch.

Scott was on his back and tried to inch away from her.

"I didn't want it to suffer any more," he whispered.

The cow kicked it again.

The slab of stone broke and fell on Scott's legs.

He screamed as his bones were completely crushed.

The cow stood on top of the slab and looked at the remains of her child at the base of the carved rock. When the incident had happened, the farmer had left the carcass to be picked apart by local wildlife. It wasn't worth the hassle to remove it, better it be left to rot.

The cow started to cry, tears streaming down her face, clearing runnels in the gore covering her nose. They hit the slab as bloody rain drops. She stepped off the slab and bent her head down again to Scott's. He was fading in and out. Her tongue flicked out and licked his face, almost as if she was cleaning her calf. He came to. The cow stared at him with her big brown eyes then stamped down on his face with her front leg, again and again until his head was mush.

A shout made her look up. Another human was coming this way. She left, deliberately walking through the thick grass to remove bits of brain from her hooves.

Scott made the news for a couple of days. *The Sun* went to town on the prospect of a "killer cow" roaming the land and how all of the first responders started vomiting at the mess when he was found by his friend. There had been a couple of tributes; from his friend, his boss and the landlord of his local boozer.

"He looked like roadkill that's been hit by a hundred cars," one anonymous source was reported to have said.

The farmer was quoted in one of the newspapers saying that the land must surely be cursed "what with that incident with the cows all dying years ago, and now this – maybe it's time for me to sell up."

When Scott's debts were settled, everything that was left went into an account that could only be accessed by Shannon on her eighteenth birthday. She also got his collection of CDs. Boxes and boxes of them arrived, courtesy of Dave, who had cleaned out Scott's flat. Tabitha wanted to get rid of them, but Shannon was adamant, they belonged to her dad, and now they belonged to *her*.

One day, on her tenth birthday, she opened up *Dead Cities* by The Future Sound of London. She took out the disc and behind it were four small squares of paper, all joined together. They had pictures of strawberries on them. She looked at it, then popped the paper into her mouth and chewed down on it.

It didn't taste of anything, certainly not strawberries. She gave the paper, Scott's long-forgotten LSD stash, another hard chew for good measure, just in case flavour would slowly rush out, like in *Charlie and the Chocolate Factory*. But no, nothing. She spat it on her palm and put it in the bin. Shannon put the disc into the player and pressed play.

ACKNOWLEDGEMENTS

This book would not have gone ahead without Trevor Kennedy, publisher and friend. Thank you for taking a chance with it, I hope it's what you wanted! Thanks to my typo tamer, Gina R. Collia. I love your bones. You're an amazing *fiend* and thanks for helping out with this wild animal!

I'd like to mention what an amazing cover this is, by the incredible artist D.N.S. His work exactly captures the spirit of the anthology and I couldn't think of a better artist for it.

Thanks also to all the authors who have written great yarns for this book. It was a pleasure to work on every story and trade thoughts and edits with writers at the top of their game.

Family Mains, as always. I love you.

Finally I'd like to thank my puppy, Lilly. She's six months old and has shat on the floor more times than I'd care to imagine, but those eyes! Those teeth! Here's to the best adventures together.

FURTHER READING

Below is a list of *personal* favourites that you might like to try and get a hold of if your tastes lie in humans getting absolutely rinsed by mother nature's finest.

Victoria Burgoyne – *Savage*
Robert Calder – *The Dogs*
Simon Ian Childer – *Worm*
Richard Curtis – *Squirm*
Robert Evans – *Croak*
Stephen Gilbert – *Willard*
John Godey – *The Snake*
Joseph L. Gilmore – *Rattlers*
Richard Haigh – *The Farm, The City*
John Halkin – *Bloodworm, Slime, Slither, Squelch*
Jessica Hamilton – *Baxter*
James Herbert – *The Rats*
Shaun Hutson – *Breeding Ground, Slugs*
David James – *Croc*
Edward Jarvis – *Maggots*
Stephen King – *Cujo*
Harry Adam Knight – *Slimer*
Richard Lewis – *The Devil's Coach-Horse, Spiders, The Web*
Edward Levy – *Came a Spider*
Michael Linaker – *Scorpion*
David Lowman – *Blowfly*
David J. Michael – *Death Tour*
James Montague – *Worms*
Pierce Nace – *Eat Them Alive*
Jack Ramsay – *The Rage*
Alan Ryan – *Panther!*

John Sayles – *Piranha*
Alan Schofield – *Venom*
Nick Sharman – *The Cats*
Andrew Sinclair – *Cat*
Nigel Slater – *The Mad Death*
Martin Cruz Smith – *Nightwing*
Guy N. Smith – *Alligators, Bats Out of Hell,
Night of the Crabs*
Mark Sonders – *Blight*
E. B. Stambaugh – *Mantis*
Donald Thompson – *The Ancient Enemy*
Peter Tremayne – *The Ants*
Cliff Twemlow – *The Beast of Kane, The Pike*

Printed in Great Britain
by Amazon